Intercepted

J. Q. Anderson

Editing by Marilyn Anderson

Cover design by Okay Creations

Formatting by Michael Stegen

To my family,
for their unconditional love and support of my wicked, naughty
and endless imagination

Intercepted

The wind brushes the snow into a cloud of dust. I squeeze my eyes, my blood pulsing in my ears.

I'm cold, so cold.

The restraints on my wrists bite into my skin as I use the last of my strength to try to break free. It's pointless. This is how it ends.

I'm going to die here.

It's depressing that the sum of the broken parts of my life has added up to this. I couldn't save Tango. I couldn't save Mom.

I can't even save myself.

I surrender to the darkness that pulls me down and let numbness invade me.

And the pain that envelopes me, begins to drift away.

Chapter 1: *Natalia*

I scan the room listlessly and my eyes lock with his. A corner of his mouth curves up like he knows something. I immediately look away. Rule number one: No getting involved with the guests.

Dani snaps me back to the present when she slides a tray filled with glasses and beer bottles onto the bar. Zack, the bartender, immediately clears them away and starts on the next order.

Zack, Daniela, and I, met during our first year of culinary school. Every summer–winter if you're in the northern hemisphere–we take a break from our lives in Buenos Aires to spend three months in Aspen, where we cater to America's wealthy after a day on the slopes.

Zack and Dani are my best friends. My only friends.

After that night, two years ago, I keep it simple: work and money. The only two things that matter now.

All in all it's pretty sweet: wake up, ski, work, smile, split the tips with Zack and Dani, ski again at night. We scored this gig because Zack knows the owner of the resort, so we get to live here, too, even though we are not full time. The three of us always get the same shift, which leaves us a couple of hours to go skiing on the one chair that's open till midnight. We've been doing it for four years. The pay is not great, but we make more money on tips than we would in three months in Buenos Aires working any other job. This is my last round, though. I graduated last month, and after this season, I'm planning to get a "real job."

"The guys on six are loaded already. The one on the left practically eye fucked me while I was taking his order. *Boludo*." Dani checks her hair in the mirror paneling the back of the bar. My eyes dart to the guy.

"Ew. He's like *fifty*."

Zack shakes his head and Dani shrugs.

"Yeah, well. He needs to hit the gym if he wants a twenty-three year old ass."

"Dani! Gross." I nudge her with my elbow. She chuckles and refills the tray with the new drinks Zack made.

Dani is a hopeless flirt. She doesn't really discriminate by age as long as the guy is good-looking and sexy. All she has to do is flick back her sandy, waist-long hair and her victims are doomed under those glacier blue eyes. She also works out diligently, so guys hit on her nonstop. She loves it.

"The guy on twelve keeps staring at you. What'd you do to him?" She laughs.

My eyes go up, and once again, I'm struck by the intensity of that look. I blush furiously and turn around to pick up my own tray, now filled with new drinks. I've seen him at night on the slopes, always by himself. He's a good skier and sort of...ugh, insanely good-looking. My cheeks warm up again.

"Nothing," I mutter defensively. Zack looks at me from the corner of his eye and chuckles.

I'm not like Dani. I'm here for the money. I've applied for a hotel management internship at a hotel in San Diego, but the cost of living in the U.S. is unreal. I almost have enough for the first four months of rent, and after this ski season, I'll have enough to carry me over until the internship ends. If things go well and I play my cards right, they will hire me afterwards, and I'll have a good paying job under the tutelage of one of the best chefs in the country.

I secure the tray on my hand and set off toward my section. Without really meaning to, I glance over at the guy to see if he's still looking. He is now focused on the people at his table. I can't help noticing everyone's expression as he speaks. He's got their full interest and seems at ease with himself. I stop at my table and smile absentmindedly as I hand out the drinks. My attention is still with the guy. I'm standing no more than two feet away from him, but he's facing the opposite way. I'm relieved by the fact that he can't see me, because by now I'm pretty much staring. For the first time, I notice he's not...alone. A perfectly groomed hand with scarlet fingernails threads in his hair at the nape and stays there, playing with the rebellious faded strands at the end. I feel an inappropriate pang of envy at the much older woman getting his attention.

Apparently, Dani is not the only one dismissing the age barrier.

He leans over casually and kisses her, but doesn't linger.

A question from a girl at my table yanks me back to the now. I blink at her in a daze because I have no idea what she just said.

"Did you get all that?" she repeats. Thank God she's not one of those stuck-up brats that are all over here. She smiles and repeats the order of food and I write it down this time.

By the time my shift ends, it's after eight and I'm dog tired, but can't wait to get on the slopes. This week seemed endless, and I'm still getting used to the change in altitude. But none of it is enough to stop me from my second passion after cooking, which is skiing. To me, the best time to hit the slopes is at night, alone.

We finish cleaning up, and I tell Dani I'm going to ski a quick run, then bed. She and Zack will stay up with some of the crew playing poker, which will soon relocate to someone's room and turn into strip poker.

I yawn as I wipe off the last table before calling it a night. There's still one more group of guys tucked in a corner. They are loud and the drinks keep coming, but it's Dani's section. She'll make good tips.

"You made it through another night." I snap my head around at the husky voice behind me. My heart momentarily freezes at the pair of golden-brown eyes that are locked on mine with a familiar intensity. It's the guy. On cue, I blush and look down at my table, wiping it again.

"Yup," I say, and I'm ridiculously uncomfortable all of a sudden.

"Do you like your job?"

I look up and this time I meet his eyes dead on, because the question seems a bit too personal for a complete stranger, then frown and push the chairs so they're flush against the table.

"I've seen you here every night," he says as a way of explanation. "And all the guys that hit on you. Must get old."

WTF? I still for a sec, absorbing the words, then shrug and pick up the rag I was cleaning with. "It's a job."

"I know the feeling," he mutters.

I glance at him and his mouth is pressed hard, his eyes lost somewhere in the pale blue glimmer of the snow outside. His features are very masculine, the straight lines of his face blending harmoniously. A slight stubble covers his face. It's kind of hot. His eyes suddenly meet mine and I curse myself inwardly for being caught staring.

"Have a nice evening," I say, tucking the tray under my arm. I dart to the bar and down the glass of water Zack always leaves for me there. My heart is pumping in a weird way. Like I just ran suicides. I resent it and will it to settle. It doesn't. Dammit. I don't need this.

"Got yourself a date?" Zack taunts without making eye contact, because he knows better. He is busy loading clean wine glasses on a rack.

I make a show of rolling my eyes and slide him the empty glass.

"Later."

"Later. Don't feel obligated to show up at the poker game. I may have a shot if you're out."

I smile as sweetly as I can manage. "We'll see."

Back in the room I share with Dani, I go straight to the closet and retrieve my ski boots, dropping them by the bed. They were a gift from Marc along with ridiculously expensive ski pants and jacket. I'm not really into clothes or expensive stuff, but I have to admit having good boots makes a huge difference. Skiing in Aspen is the ultimate treat. Zack is an instructor in Argentina during the winter, and over the last three years taught me everything I know. Now I go pretty much everywhere on the mountain, including double black diamonds. All except one. The Women's Downhill.

Not since the accident. The thought makes me shudder and I immediately close the door on it. I slip into my UGGS–those I bought for myself– and head out for a well-deserved late-night run.

Chapter 2: *Jake*

It's eleven and Tamara is already asleep. Stretching out on an armchair by the window of the suite she paid for, I watch the trail of glimmering lights outlining the ski slopes while I nurse my scotch. I glance at my watch. The night chair will be open till midnight. I consider going for a quick run, then decide against it when a sharp stab on my quad reminds me of the fall I took last night. I've been skiing after Tamara goes to sleep every evening, and yesterday the moon was full, so I ventured off the trail and into a path of virgin powder. It was incredible. The feeling of almost floating, every muscle in my legs burning, every part of me alive. I caught an edge towards the end and it earned me an almost torn quad. Tamara doesn't know because she thinks I was here, sleeping next to her. I told her I strained it the next morning when we were skiing together and she believed me. She always believes me and doesn't ask any questions.

I glance in her direction and watch her sleep for a moment. She looks peaceful, young, even though she's more than a decade older than me. Like most women I'm with, Tamara takes good care of her body. She's got incredible legs and a pair of tits that would put any twenty year old out of the race in a second. I look back through the window and focus on the lift, which has now stopped.

I down the last of my scotch and shrug into a jacket, determined to find a way to pass the next few hours, 'cause I know sleeping is off the table. Earlier, I heard one of the waiters talk about a late poker game within the hotel staff, so I'm gonna find out where it is.

I follow the hallway into the main lobby, which is now deserted save an employee behind the front desk doing paperwork. Without letting him see me, I head to the bar I was in with Tamara a few hours back, but the lights are dim. The room looks cavernous. Through the black windows, the moon bathes the snow outside. There are a couple of guys at a table in the back and they look drunk as fuck.

I amble through the main areas, but there are no signs of anything. Maybe I should go ask the guys running the ski lift. I dart a look outside and see they're packing up. Grabbing my beanie out of my pocket, I slide it over my head and push the side door that leads out to Needle, the night chair. Arctic air claws my face the second I step out and I take a big pull of it, welcoming the burn in my lungs. It's tinted with tobacco and I turn my head toward the source of the smell. A guy in his early twenties flashes me a quick smile before taking another puff of his cigarette. He's wearing a heavy jacket over a bell uniform. His face looks vaguely familiar.

"Want a smoke?" He pulls a packet out of his pocket.

I don't smoke, but this guy may be my ticket to that poker game, so I reach for it and put a cigarette between my lips. He pulls a lighter and flicks it, cupping the flame with his hand.

"Thanks." I take a drag and immediately regret it. How people can be addicted to this shit is beyond me.

"You've been up in Needles?" He gestures to the lift with his chin. His black hair covers most of his forehead. He flicks it with a quick snap of his head.

"Nah. Not tonight. Taking the night off."

He nods, then extends his hand. "I'm Shane." He has a broad, easy smile.

"Jake." I bring the cigarette to my mouth to free my hand and shake his.

"I've seen you around. You're the one with that...blond gal." The corner of his mouth curves up as he says it.

I shake my head and chuckle. "Yeah."

The sound of packing snow saves me from that conversation when two guys from the lift walk in our direction. I recognize one of them from the last couple of nights when I went skiing. He makes quick eye contact with me and nods, then flashes a smile to Shane.

"Ready for me to kick your ass again? Hope you made good tips today, man. You're gonna need them." He grins.

"*Kiss* my ass, Derek. I'm gonna get it all back and go home with your tips, too, asshole."

Derek chuckles loudly and gives him the finger as he shuffles to the entrance.

"Can you guys use one more?" I put out my cigarette pretending I don't really care either way. But for some reason I do. I need this. Derek stops in his tracks and locks eyes with me, then looks at Shane. Shane shrugs.

"Fine with me."

Derek darts one last look at me. "Private game, sorry," he mutters.

"Wouldn't you rather make more money? I'm not very good." I do my best to sound unaffected. He meets my eyes dead on.

"Look, man, you're a guest. Your kind don't mix with ours." Something dark crosses his eyes. He's about to head for the door when I lift my hand, so he stops.

"I'll give you two hundred bucks each if you let me in. Just for tonight. It can still be a private game. I'd rather keep it that way anyway." What the fuck. Did I just offer these two assholes four hundred bucks for a fucking poker game? I clench my teeth. I guess I fucking need this more than I thought.

Shane scoffs. "Seriously?"

"Yeah," I answer without looking at him. My eyes are still locked with Derek's.

"I'm in, Derek." Shane takes one last draw of his cigarette, then steps on it.

Derek gives me a quick nod. "Just for tonight."

Chapter 3: *Natalia*

When I unlock the door to my room, it's after midnight. Dani is not here. I'm guessing she's already at the poker game. I send her a quick text asking her where it is and she responds almost instantly with a room number. I don't really feel like staying up, but I can use the money. Poker is one of those things I learned when I was young. I'm good at it. While other girls hung out in their lame little clique groups, I sat behind the gym building with Tango acquiring valuable poker skills.

Tango was my best friend and by far the smartest person I've ever met. His dad was a mean drunk, so most days he hung out at our apartment. Mom always found excuses to make him stay. She loved him as if he were her own, and I know for a fact she would have adopted him if we could have afforded to. The memories churn in my chest and I shut the door on them.

I knock on room 244, in the wing of the hotel assigned to the staff. While I wait, I make sure nobody's around. These games are obviously not permitted on the hotel premises, which is why they change locations every time.

Shane, from the bell department/ opens the door and lets me in, flashing an easy smile. He looks so much younger in street clothes. I give him a quick hug as I walk in. Dani waves from the other side of the round table where the game is already in full swing under a cloud of smoke. Zack is sitting next to her. His eyes meet mine and he groans, mumbling something about his chances going out the window. I do a quick sweep of the faces. Two guys I don't know, then my breath hitches when I see Hot Guy from the restaurant sitting next to Dani. He looks up and smiles broadly as recognition crosses his eyes. *Fuckdammit*. I no longer remember how to breathe. *In. Out. In. Out. Come on, Natalia. You've done this all your life.*

Shane defrosts me when he tells me I can take the spot next to Derek, who's sitting opposite Dani. Hot Guy's eyes don't leave mine as I take a seat across from him. Something in my stomach flutters. I don't know why his presence makes me so uneasy. I work with lots of guys, my first friend was a guy, and as far as flirting I'm not even on the market because I'm engaged. Maybe that's it. The way this guy's eyes are locked into mine seems...indecent.

I shake off the discomfort in my stomach and focus on the cards I was dealt. Not much, but I have all night to make these guys think my skills are rusty. There are eight people at the table, including me, and I have beat every single one of them in the past, except the new guys. This is the first game of the season and if things go well, it will add a nice bonus to my overall income.

"It's a five card draw and you need fifty to be in," Derek says as he deals. I fish a fifty out of my pocket and lay it on the table.

"Is this game expanding?" I glance at the two new guys before pausing slightly on Hot Guy.

Derek shrugs. "That's Pete, snowboard instructor; Liam bartends at the Spyglass bar, and that's...Jake. He's...not with the staff, but it's cool."

I nod slightly. *Dammit.* Now he has a name. A cool one.

"Hi again. I'm Jake." He smiles and it's like someone just sucked the wind out of my lungs.

"Natalia." I nod once. "Aren't you a guest?" I look at my cards, then back at him, doing my best to sound impassive. I cannot let this guy mess with my mojo.

"Yeah, but it's past my bedtime, so I'm not even here." He winks and for some reason it feels intimate. I look away at Dani to shake off the feeling. She winks, too. *Shit.* I focus on Zack and he narrows his eyes at me.

"I thought you were tired. Don't you need a night off?"

I smile at him and scrunch my nose as I study my cards.

"Nah. Need to build up the pot."

Zack lets out another one of his groans. "You'll be tired and moody tomorrow. I won't let you take it out on me. Especially after taking my goddamn money."

"Aww, such little faith in yourself, Zacky."

He mumbles something unintelligible and I blow him a kiss.

The game is on and I wait a few rounds, letting the others play their hands while I wait for the right moment. Two hours pass and only Zack, Derek, Jake and I remain in the game. The stakes are high. A little over two hundred dollars are piled in the center of the table, mostly tens and fives given that the source was tips.

Zack has nothing and Derek's luck isn't much better. Jake raises an eyebrow and lays his full house on the table. I smile inwardly, but don't move a muscle. Tango was a good teacher.

"Those are good," I mutter.

"How good?" His eyes are locked on mine and it's as if an electric field has formed around us. The room is a vacuum.

All eyes are on me.

I purse my lips, the first facial expression I allow myself and shake my head slightly, then lower my cards and gently slide them on the table.

My straight flush beats his full house and I meet his eyes dead on with a wide grin.

He narrows his eyes, but a hint of a smile curves up a corner of his mouth.

"Damn." He looks at my cards and shakes his head, like he still can't believe it.

Dani cheers and hugs me from behind. Zack slides his chair back and runs both hands through his hair, then stretches.

"I don't know why I bother. I should just give you the money." He gets up and darts me a sulky look before walking out the door. I smile because I know he can't stay mad and he'll go back to being nice to me tomorrow.

Dani gathers the bills, organizing them in a single pile. She's a master at it and works quickly. She loves helping me because my wins mean we go shopping. She knows I'll buy her something nice. She would do the same for me, but she's only won twice last season...on nights I wasn't playing.

"You're good," Jake extends his hand to shake mine. "Didn't see you coming." I shake his hand and immediately regret it. His hand completely envelopes mine. It is strong, a bit callused, definitely not what I would have expected from a guy vacationing in Aspen with a Barbie girlfriend. The image of her hand in his hair trespasses my thoughts. She looked older than him and I'm intrigued. My hand is still in his and I pull it away, the skin-to-skin contact strangely lacking the second I let go.

"Thanks. I'll see you around." I look at Dani who has finished packing the bills in her bag. She does a little victory dance in front of Derek and Shane, who shake their heads but laugh anyway. Derek calls it a night and kicks everyone out of his room. Jake turns in the direction of the guest area while Shane, Dani, and I, head toward our rooms at the opposite end of the hallway.

Before I follow Dani into the room, I turn my head around to see Jake standing at his end of the hallway. Our eyes lock for a moment and the unwelcome feeling in my stomach returns full force. With a single, quick wave, he turns away. I close the door behind me and lean against it.

Shit.

Chapter 4: *Jake*

I enter silently so I don't wake Tamara. She stirs and I still, but then she rolls over and I relax. I don't think she'd care that I've been out, but I don't like explaining myself to anyone. Haven't done that since I was eight.

I lie in bed next to her, unable to sleep. All I can see when I close my eyes are those fierce green eyes and that untamed mane of endless black hair. *Natalia.* She's sexy as fuck and I know it will be a challenge to be around her the next few days when I'm supposed to give all my attention to Tamara. I remind myself that this is a work week for me and I can't let distractions like Natalia fuck with work. But I close my eyes and she's there, barging into my mind, pouting her mouth in that sexy way that went straight to my dick. Her mouth is perfect. It taunts me even in my sleep. I dream about pinning her against the jacuzzi wall, smothering her mouth while I fuck her.

She moans...*Christ.*

Tamara's warm body pressed to mine awakes me. Her hand finds my dick, and she lets out a pleased groan because I'm already hard. Without opening my eyes, I roll over on top of her, spreading her legs with mine. She giggles and grinds her hips against mine. Natalia's face filters into my thoughts and I keep my eyes closed, holding onto the image as I thrust into Tamara. It's intense, unusually mind-blowing and even though I don't understand the hold this girl has on me I go with it. Tamara cries out loud and I come hard with only one image in my head. *Natalia.*

This week's shaping up differently than I thought.

In the morning Tamara and I ride the chair to the top of the mountain. It's not too crowded up high, so we are able to get a few runs in. It feels good to get my blood flowing. Tamara is a good skier and has no trouble catching up with me. Most women I go out with are barely average, so I'm enjoying this part of our trip. We have lunch at the Spyglass bar, a secluded spot overlooking the whole valley. I recognize one of the guys from last night...Liam, I think. He nods at me and I give him a brief nod back.

After lunch, Tamara says she's tired and wants to take a nap. At the base, the valet meets us to take our boots.

"Are you sure you don't mind if I go see Keira this evening?" Tamara runs her fingernails through my hair as I pull on my after-ski boots. I give her an impassive smile although I'm more than glad to have time alone.

"Of course not. Have fun, babe."

She slides onto my lap and wraps her arms around my neck. "What are you going to do on your evening off, all alone?"

"I'll swim a few laps. My legs feel tight."

She pouts. "You'll be at the pool without me? I don't know if I like that. I saw the way those waitresses were looking at you."

"Tamara. You know you don't need to worry about that. This week I'm yours, babe." I kiss her and she smiles against my lips.

"That's right. This week is *mine*. Maybe you'll even get a bonus if you manage to not get distracted."

I pull my head back. "I don't get distracted."

She smiles and slides off my lap. I know she's pleased with herself for reminding me of the boundaries. I let her because in the end, she's nothing to me but another job.

Vapor hovers over the heated pool, the surface invisible under a layer of fog. It is close to midnight and the pool area is deserted. I shrug off my robe and stand at the edge, pausing to take in the incredible peace that surrounds me, then I lower my goggles and dive into the water. This is the best part. Those five seconds after my body first meets the water. The cathartic, cleansing feeling of the world washing off me. I close my eyes and drift back to my life at the ranch with Dad and my brother Jamie. When I was free, and the minutes in my life weren't paid for by someone else.

I reach the end and flip-turn into the next lap. The familiar burn spreads through my muscles and I welcome it. I try to clear my mind, but Natalia's image haunts me. This sucks because thinking about women is not something I spend any time doing. My life is simple and I like it that way. But this girl, something about her lures me in and I want to know who she is. She had an accent. Maybe Italian. *Fuck, Jake.* I switch to butterfly to engage every single cell and drown all thoughts of her.

Chapter 5: *Natalia*:

I plop onto the bed face down. My shift was totally shitty. I can deal with annoying, rich customers and it's all good because the tips are great, but the drunk creeps that stay at the bar until we close get on my nerves.

I'm too tired to go skiing. Maybe the jacuzzi. My cell phone vibrates in my pocket, startling me. Marc's sleepy voice makes me smile.

"Hey."

"Hey. Perfect timing. Just ended my shift." I reach for a pillow and get comfy.

"Got your pockets full of numbers from hot, single guys who want you to call them?"

I chuckle. "Yeah. Just sitting here deciding…"

"I miss you baby."

I miss him, too. I close my eyes and imagine he's lying next to me.

"I want to see you. When can you come?" I yawn.

"A week from Friday."

I frown. "I thought maybe you'd come this weekend."

"Baby, I can't. I'm going to have to work all weekend for a pitch I have on Monday."

"Okay." I let out an exasperated sigh.

Our conversation doesn't last long because we are both tired and frankly, I'm getting frustrated that we are apart. Our long distance relationship is getting harder and harder to endure. I hate that he lives so far away. He's been flying down to Buenos Aires pretty much once a month, thanks to his generous income as a creative director in advertising. I'm a brat for complaining, but it's still frustrating.

I kick off my shoes and chat with a friend via text for a while, then she says she has to leave for the movies and I'm left solo again. Our room is small and I don't want to hang out here. Dani is out with Zack having drinks in someone's room and I could join them, but I need a break from everyone at work. I get my butt off the bed and decide to pay the jacuzzi a visit.

The gelid night air hits me as I walk out the side door leading to the pool. It's deserted except for a lane where a guy is swimming laps. I pull the collar of my robe around me to block the chill. It still smells like Marc and I smile. I remember telling him I was stealing it because I wanted his scent on me every morning. Dipping my head, I meander in the direction of the jacuzzi. I'm still a good distance away when my eyes pause on the swimmer. There is something beautiful, almost poetic, about the way his body flows with the water. It's also magnetic because I can't look away. As I move closer, I notice he's in really good shape. He's swimming in a rhythmic butterfly stroke. His back bobs in and out of the water and I fixate on the outline of every muscle. He stops at the end and turns, leaning on the edge as he takes a break.

I skid to a halt. *Shit.*

Jake.

He slides up his goggles and meets my surely blanched expression with a grin. *Dammit.* I give him a half wave and set off in the direction I was heading before he short-circuited my thoughts.

He lifts himself out with astonishing ease, then sits on the edge, letting his legs dangle into the water. It's like the laws of gravity don't apply because he did it in one seamless movement. He's still smiling and looks as if he's about to say something. *Crap.* I don't want to engage in a conversation with him. Something about him makes me uneasy. I'm also trying to avoid looking at his body because...well, because it's fucking perfect, that's why.

"Couldn't sleep?" His voice is low and sort of raspy. I don't want to think about his voice.

"Yeah." I shrug, trying to look non-committal. Maybe if he thinks I'm boring he'll leave me alone. "Just heading for the jacuzzi."

He nods and I think I'm off the hook, but his eyes are still on me. I try to shake it off and turn toward the jacuzzi area behind him. If he makes a move I'll keep walking and go to my room because the fact that we are the only two people here is making me uncomfortable. He dives back into the pool and I relax.

In the jacuzzi, I close my eyes and let my body melt into the enveloping heat of the water, welcoming the contrast with the nipping air over the surface. It's not long before my face is beaded with sweat. I lower my head all the way into the water to wash it off. When I come up, Jake is standing at the edge of the jacuzzi.

Fuckdammit.

My heart ninja kicks my chest. I push myself back and grip the edge behind me.

"Sorry," he chuckles, and it's so addictive I can't think straight. "I didn't mean to startle you. Mind if I hop in? I just need to wind down."

I shake my head No, still unable to formulate a coherent sentence. Up this close he looks like something Michelangelo took a decade to sculpt. It hurts to swallow because my mouth is completely dry.

"Long shift?" He smiles briefly as he eases himself into the jacuzzi, letting out a pleased groan that hits a forgotten spot inside me.

"Yes, long."

He studies me and says nothing. His eyelashes are endless and still wet, and...I want to leave. He's freaking hot and it's bugging me how aware I am of it. I have a fiancé for fuck's sake.

"I'm beat." He sighs and runs a hand through his long, straight hair. It was sandy brown yesterday, but I can't help noticing how good it looks now, darker because it's wet. His eyes are liquid caramel. Every part of him is well taken care of and it makes me automatically assume he's probably full of himself.

"How does it feel?" The words are out of my mouth and I frown, like they've betrayed me.

He tilts his head to the side. "How does what feel?"

I curse myself inwardly, but now it's done. "Swimming."

He angles his head a bit more and looks at me like I just spoke in another language. I shrug.

"I'm wondering, because you swim really well and I...well, I can't swim at all. So watching someone in the water like that sort of blows me away." *Shit*. That just sounded like I was flirting. I glance at my watch to feign disinterest.

He doesn't speak right away and now I really want to leave because his silence reassures me he thinks that was a pickup line.

"It feels incredible," he finally says. "Like you leave everything behind and nothing can touch you."

A pang of envy flicks in my chest. I ignore it and nod. "Where did you learn?"

"I played water polo in college, then professionally for a few years after."

I hate that I think what he just said is super cool. It adds up. The ripped back, the aerodynamic fusion between his body and the water. I stretch my legs and swirl my toes so I'm not looking at him so much.

"Not anymore?" I ask, pretending my toes are more interesting.

"Not anymore." He doesn't say anything else and it makes me look straight at him. A flash of regret crosses his eyes, but it's gone almost immediately. His eyes scan the landscape behind me, then meet mine full force.

"So what's your story, Natalia?"

I open my mouth and close it. I'm trying to stop the craze caused to my vitals when he said my name. I hate how great he made sound the word I've heard every day since I can remember. I look away, gathering my wits.

"Um…there's not much to tell. I live in Buenos Aires, I just graduated from college and I come here in the summer…well, winter for you, and work the season." That's all I say because I'm not interested in making a new friend. Especially a hot one that looks at me the way he's looking at me right now. Those eyes are seriously flirting with my pulse and I cannot let that happen.

"I think there's much more to tell than you let on," he says in that same hoarse, low tone. "I learned it in that poker game last night. You took every penny I had."

That makes me grin. I'm not beyond pride when it comes to my poker abilities.

"Do you want to go out one night?"

WTF? My jaw drops. I know he knows I saw him with that middle-aged Barbie. I narrow my eyes.

"Your girlfriend doesn't mind you asking other women out on dates?" My tone is caustic and I think it takes him off guard. Then realization crosses his eyes and he relaxes.

"Tamara is not my girlfriend. And she's leaving tomorrow."

I shake my head. These rich guys are all the same. Women are just tools to them.

"Thank you, Jake. But I'm not interested. And even if I was, I'm sure my fiancé would not be happy with that. I gotta go." I start to stand up, but his hand catches mine and stops me. I stare at him, ignoring the head-to-toe chills caused by the skin to skin contact, and pull my hand away.

"I'm sorry. I didn't mean to offend you. Stay."

I give him a long look. I should probably go back to my room, but my body is on strike with my mind and refuses to move. Besides, the warm water feels so damn good. I look away, abandoning the impulse to leave. I assure myself Jake has nothing to do with my decision.

I slip back into the water and keep a safe distance from him. But the fact that we are here alone makes this feel more intimate than I'm comfortable with. I stay mainly quiet as he tells me about his life at a ranch in Santa Barbara, where he grew up. It kind of bugs me that he's so easy to talk to. Something about him commands my attention as he slowly wears down my guard. He speaks as if we've known each other for a lifetime, laughing out loud as he recalls the memories he's sharing with me. He talks about his younger brother and his dad and the horses. He doesn't mention his mom and I don't ask. Not because I'm not curious, my interest is piqued, but I hate it when people ask me about my mom. An image of her braiding my hair flashes in my mind and the bitterness of losing her to cancer so early unfurls and surfaces. *I couldn't save her.* I smother the memory. When I look up, Jake has stopped talking and is watching me with an amused expression.

"Where'd you go?

"What?" I frown.

He tilts his head and smiles. I now realize this is a habit of his. Tilting his head to the side as a corner of his mouth curls up. *Dammit.* I'm staring at his mouth again. His smile widens and suddenly I'm blushing beet red and I cannot get out of this jacuzzi fast enough. What the hell am I doing here with this guy?

"You're leaving?" He sounds disappointed and it makes me smile because it's just...well. *Damn hot*.

"Yeah. I'm spent. I'll see you around, I guess."

He gives me a brief nod, a ghost of a smug smile playing on his lips. "See you around, *Natalia*."

I close my eyes for a second, glad he can't see me because my back is turned, and let the sound of my name trickle through me. I don't know what it is that sounds different when he says it. Maybe it's the fact that he lingers on the "t" a tad too long, his tongue *tsks* behind his teeth, making it sound almost...Italian. Or maybe it's my fucking girl hormones telling me it's been way too long since I last saw Marc.

I scurry away and don't stop until I reach the glass doors leading to the employee wing. Before I push through, I turn my head. His eyes are still on me and he grins.

Dammit.

Chapter 6: *Jake*

The moment she closes the door, I start the countdown until I see her again. Tamara will leave in the morning and it doesn't seem soon enough. I curse myself inwardly for caving into the spell Natalia's put on me. Since when do I let a woman infiltrate my thoughts? I know I've got to get a fucking grip, but the anticipation for another encounter with her builds as the minutes pass, knowing that come tomorrow I'll have free range to do whatever I want without the nuisances of my job.

She said she has a fiancé and I can't help a stab of anger. I suddenly have to know what the fucker looks like and what I'm up against. *Up against? Christ, get a hold of yourself, Jake.* Right. First I have to know if she'd be game. I don't have work commitments for the next two weeks and...Fuck. I already sound like a stalker. But I know that if I turn my back on whatever is pulling me to Natalia, I'll be left wondering. I have to know what the fuck this is. Even if it means breaking the rules. I need to recover the peace of mind that comes with being in control. By no means am I interested in a relationship. I just need my brain to stop imagining her naked body rocking against mine.

I head back to my room and when I unlock the door Tamara is getting into bed, naked. My dick would normally stir at the sight of her sculpted body, but instead, I'm wishing she was already gone. *Fuck, Jake. Snap out of it.* She smiles, pleased to see me.

"Did you have a good workout? I hope you're not too tired." Her smile widens and I can't help the sudden dread that fills me.

One more night. I'm pissed at my lack of restraint toward my rebellious mind, and give her an appraising look.

"If I'm ever too tired for you, then there'd be something seriously wrong with me, babe." I smile and she throws her head back in laugher, pleased with herself.

"Come here," she says, extending her hand.

I rid myself of the towel and swim trunks and get into bed, fighting against my now foul mood. *Get a fucking grip, Jake.*

Luck is on my side. Tamara confesses she drank too much with her friend. I fuck her with my eyes closed, and I don't think she cares. It doesn't take her long to come and I'm relieved. She rolls over and is immediately asleep, unaware I didn't get there. Normally this would piss me off, but tonight I don't care because my thoughts are with that sable-haired girl I can't get out of my mind.

The next morning I fuck Tamara in the shower before she leaves. I don't even want to admit where my mind was as I slammed into her until she collapsed, exhausted, in my arms. But it made for a satisfying start of the day. It also made the urge to find Natalia prevail over everything else. It both pleases me and pisses me off.

"The room is paid for till tomorrow," Tamara croons, her arms hanging around my neck as she kisses me goodbye one last time. "I figured you'd like having a day to rest before going back."

"Thank you, babe. That's very generous." I give her a sideways smile and kiss her.

"Will you be in Santa Monica for the next couple of weeks? Maybe we can do another weekend." Her blue eyes assess me. I contemplate the possibility for a moment, then follow my gut and lie. She's starting to get clingy.

"No, babe. I'm not." I don't explain further. She knows the boundaries. I don't talk about my schedule or my personal life with clients. I see the hurt cross her eyes, but I remain unaffected.

"Okay. See you soon then." She smiles. I give her one last kiss before she gets into the taxi that'll take her to the airport.

"Goodbye, Jake."

I watch her leave, then turn to the lodge.

Game on.

I stride back into the lobby, my eyes sweeping across the lounge as I pass. I know she's still not there. Her shifts are nights. I'm starting to feel like a creep, but I only have one day left to put my mind at ease and assure myself Natalia is no different from the other women I've met: manipulative and fucking deceitful. But I have to know for sure. And time is running out quick.

Says who?

Hmm. I actually don't *have* to be back. The next two weeks I'm free. I stop at the lounge entrance. The bartender and a busboy are setting up for the lunch shift. He looks up, acknowledging me with a nod. I nod back and scan the room, but there are no signs of Natalia. Maybe it's her day off. *Shit.* I feel like an asshole, obsessing over a girl I barely know. Reminding myself she has a fucking fiancé, I shake my head and stride to my room. I decide to hit the slopes to rid my body and mind of the irrational thoughts that haunt me.

At the summit, the mountain is silent. The fog is so thick I can't even make out the outline of my skis. I lower my goggles and speed off. I need this. Feel the burn in my muscles. The exhilaration that comes from skiing at blinding speed.

The snow is shit. I hit ice as I fly down a double black diamond and almost lose my balance when I catch an edge. The jagged end of a tree branch grazes my forehead with a sting. As I get off the trail, I hit a long patch of powder. It makes the shitty morning worth it, and for the next two hours my mind is only on the trail ahead.

By the time I call it a day, I'm wiped out. I hand my ski boots to the valet, eager for food and a shower. He tells me I'm bleeding and it takes me a few seconds to realize he's referring to the scrape on my forehead. I wipe it off with a tissue I find in my pocket.

In my room, I open my laptop and check email while I wait for room service. It's been almost a week since I sent the modifications to the plans for the surf shop to the contractor, but he still hasn't responded. We need all the permits cleared so we can close the deal on that open spot by Cardiff Beach in San Diego. I fire off another email to him, stressing that we're pressed on time, and letting him know I expect an answer in the next 24 hours. He better get on this if he wants to keep his job.

My food arrives and I'm famished. I make quick work of devouring it, then take a shower. Free of all the tension from this morning, I stand by the massive window and stare at the receding fog. What the fuck am I after here…I should leave tomorrow and use the free time I have to find a place to live in San Diego. If everything moves forward and I open the surf shop, commuting to Santa Monica is out of the question. My mind wanders to my father. He would be pleased to know I'll have something to call my own. I drown that thought.

Shaking off the irrational impulse of staying, I pack my bag and get ready to check out the next morning. Without much left to do, I decide to go for a short swim and relax at the jacuzzi, knowing Natalia will most likely be working or having a day off and I won't risk running into her.

I swim a few laps, enjoying the fact that the fog chased off the usual guests I see here. The fatigue from this morning's skiing pulls at my muscles and I call it a night. I leap off and slip into the steaming jacuzzi, letting my body unwind.

Chapter 7: *Natalia*:

I hang up and throw my phone on the bed. Dani glances up from her laptop and gives me a wary look.

"What was that all about?"

"Shit. *Shit.*" I sit down on the bed and drop my face on my hands.

"Nati!" she scolds. I meet her expectant eyes.

"The hotel, in San Diego." I sigh in irritation. "They were just calling to confirm I got into the internship. They want me to start April second."

"How is that *not* great news?"

"Because I'll start in the kitchen, but the internship is in general hotel management and the hotel wants all their interns to be able to rotate between departments. I guess it's part of the program."

"And?"

"Including the *pool*," I mutter.

"Oh." Her expression falls.

"Shit, Dani. What am I going to do? This internship is my ticket to finally doing something on my own. I can't let this go."

"How did you not know about the pool before now?"

"I was desperate to get in. I just answered yes to all the requirements and hoped I wouldn't get that one. But it's on the list they just gave me. The lady on the phone said the pool is only a backup for the lifeguard on duty, and that I can get a CPR certification while I'm there. *Shit.*"

"Maybe you can get a pass. Maybe it's not a big deal to skip that one rotation, or they can switch it to something else."

"Maybe, but Dani, there were over a hundred people trying to get this spot. It was a miracle I got in. If I show them I'm inadequate before I even start, I'll lose the shot at getting a job there afterwards."

She scratches the back of her head. "There's gotta be something we can do. Maybe Zack can think of something. He knows everyone here. Maybe he can get you lessons with the swim instructor." Just as she says that, Zack walks in. "Speak of the devil," Dani grins.

"What?" Zack nods.

"Natalia needs swimming lessons. Can you hook her up?"

He shrugs. "Maybe. They only have Tyler now. Not much demand for swimming lessons in the winter."

"Can you ask him?" I plead. "I can't do the internship unless I can swim." My throat thickens. Even if Zack is able to help me, that would mean getting in the water and, oh yeah, fucking learn how to swim in a little over a month. What the hell am I thinking? Zack sees the change in my expression and promises to pull whatever strings he can. I hug him tight as he tells me everything will be alright, and I make myself believe it's true. He pats my back and turns to Dani.

"I actually came to tell you two that they've switched tonight's shift for the lunch tomorrow."

"What?" Dani scowls. "What the hell? Why?" The lunch tips are not even half of what we make in the evening, courtesy of the drunk slobs that can't see straight by the time the bill comes.

"They're closing the lounge tonight. I guess one of the pipes underground is leaking and they have to fix it before it bursts."

"Dammit." Dani sighs.

"There's a game in Derek's room at ten." Zack's eyes dart to mine. "Everyone needs a partner."

I give him a nod. "As long as Dani's okay with it. I already owe you, so if it's good with her it's a Yes."

Dani shakes her head. "It's fine. I'm out. I need to study for the Econ final. I'm already behind."

I give her an empathetic look. Dani still has two finals left to take in Buenos Aires. I don't push because I know she needs to study if she wants to graduate in May.

"Are you sure you want in?" Zack eyes me skeptically. "You seem a bit distracted and I'm counting on my wins tonight."

I narrow my eyes. "Are you doubting me?"

"Nope." He raises his palms in apology. "Just making sure. See you guys later. I'm smashed from last night. I'm gonna take a nap."

I leave Dani studying and go to the gym to burn off the adrenaline from the call. What the hell will I do? The only water I tolerate is a steaming jacuzzi. I trick my mind into thinking it's no different than a bath, but getting inside a real life swimming pool is a different story. The Wombats blast from my headphones, the only effective way to shut up my mind as I sprint on the treadmill with my eyes closed.

Once I have nothing else to give, I take a quick shower and set off to the jacuzzi to unwind. I wonder if Zack had time to talk to Tyler, and if he's willing to help. I text Zack and he tells me to hang on. My phone rings as I'm about to step outside into the pool area. It's Zack. My heart jackhammers my ribs.

"So? Will he do it?"

"Sorry, babe. Tyler's leaving tomorrow."

"Shit, no. Is there anyone else?" Desperation creeps to my throat.

"No. They're closing up for the season. They won't have another lifeguard till the spring."

"Fuckdammit." I slide down against the wall and put my head between my knees. "What am I going to do, Zack? I can't lose this internship."

He tells me we'll figure something out. Zack is not a great swimmer, but he says he can teach me some basics. I know that won't cut it, but I thank him anyway.

The instant I push through the doors I regret it. I immediately recognize the outline of the only body emerging from the steaming surface of the jacuzzi.

Jake.

Goddamn my luck today. I decide I don't give a crap. Dani is studying in our room, which means if I go back there, I'll have to be quiet. Zack is off to buy booze with Derek, so it's either the jacuzzi or the ski runs in the fog. To hell with it.

When I'm only a few steps away, he raises his head and opens his eyes, then frowns. What the hell is his problem? This area is open to employees too, buddy. Tough luck if you don't approve. His eyes appraise me up and down and I immediately feel self-conscious. *Shit.* Is he checking me out? Since there's not a chance in hell I'm going in the pool, my options are slim. I avoid his eyes and slide into the water, hooking my earphones on so he knows I'm not up for a conversation either.

"You don't have to work?"

I can't hear him, but I can't help the fact that my eyes are always glued to his mouth and I just read his lips. *Dammit.* I turn the volume down a tad.

"Nope. Change of shift."

He nods, his eyes never leaving mine.

"What's the matter?" he says.

Now I'm ticked off. Seriously, what does he care?

"Shitty day," I mutter, closing my eyes, mainly because looking at him is distracting. He's got a fresh scrape across his forehead and I wonder how it got there. Did he dodge a tree branch when he was skiing? Maybe his Barbie girlfriend is a bit psycho and they got into a fight because she caught him flirting with the staff. I giggle at the thought, not realizing I just did it out loud.

"Something funny?" He raises an eyebrow. *Cocky bastard.* I scowl.

"How come you're always here alone? Didn't you come with someone?"

"That's why you're giggling?"

I shake my head. "No. Forget it."

"Are you always this rude to people you barely know?" He frowns.

This catches me off guard. But he's right. I'm being short and downright rude, and he doesn't deserve it. "I'm sorry." I keep my eyes on him and he relaxes, looking a bit puzzled. I think he wasn't expecting an apology.

"Why was your day shitty?" he asks. I stare at my hands under the water to avoid looking into those endless caramel eyes.

"I love to cook," I say with a half-smile. "My biggest dream is to open a place of my own someday. Nothing big, just a little place somewhere by the beach."

"That's a good dream," he says. When I look up, his frown is gone and his eyes are smiling at me.

"It is. And I was on my way to get it, too. I have an internship lined up in San Diego at a hotel in Coronado. They have the best pastry chef there. That's my favorite thing." I smile. "Pastries. They called me today and said the internship requires rotations throughout the hotel. Including lifeguarding the pool." I look up at him and he frowns, then understanding crosses his face.

"And you can't swim."

"I can't swim," I mutter.

"Just have someone here work with you. I'm sure this place has plenty of resources. That swimming instructor that walks around here. What's his name…"

"Tyler," I say with a sad smile. "He's leaving tomorrow until the spring."

"Hmm. I see." He frowns.

"I was so close. I've been interviewing for this internship for almost a year. It could lead to a job there afterwards. I have saved every penny I made so I can rent an apartment. I thought of everything...Now this."

"You're not giving up, are you?" His frown deepens. I glare up at him. His comment stings. I'm not a quitter.

"Of course not, but didn't you hear me? I can't fucking swim. I get a panic attack if I so much step inside a pool."

His eyebrows shoot up in surprise. "Um. You're sitting in one right now."

"It's different." I shake my head. "A jacuzzi is just a bigger version of a bath tub."

"So is a swimming pool." He tilts his head to the side in that way. I have to look away.

"I can't," I mutter. "It's just...different, okay?"

"Did something happen to you? Why are you afraid of water?"

I don't look at him. I just stare at the steam raising from the surface as the memory barges in my head. Panic lances through me and every one of my muscles tenses at once. *'I've got you.'* Tango's voice echoes clear in my mind. *'I won't let go, I promise.'* Tears swim in my eyes.

"I fell in a pool when I was young. It was dark, cold. So cold." I pick up my knees and hug them, the chill expanding from within. I squeeze my eyes to shut out the memory. His hand startles me when it wraps around my arm.

"I'm sorry. It's alright now."

When I look up, he's right next to me, his eyes warm. For the first time I notice they're not a solid brown. Speckles of green and gold spread out from his irises, like sun rays. They are beautiful. "I'm screwed," I whisper, unable to look away.

"I'll teach you," he says. "I'll teach you how to swim."

I straighten up. "What? You can't."

"Why not?'

"You're a guest. Besides, what about your girlfriend? Isn't this like...your vacation?"

"I told you. Tamara is not my girlfriend. And she's gone."

"Oh. What are you still doing here?"

He shrugs. "I like skiing."

I watch him for a moment, wondering what he does for a living. Whatever it is must pay well if he can afford skiing here. I refrain from the urge to ask and give him a nod.

"Look," he says. "I'm staying for two more nights. Then I'll fly home for the week, but I'm meeting some friends back here the following weekend for a guy's trip. We can work on the basics before I leave, then see where you're at when I'm back." He says it like it's all so simple. It makes me want to punch that smug expression off his face. We are talking about teaching a person who cannot get inside water under 80 degrees how to swim in just a few days. Is he serious?

"Okay?" he says.

"I...you don't even know me." Is all I'm able to say, because it's true. Why is he doing this?

"I want to help." He smiles, answering my thought. "I know what it's like to want something that much. I can help you."

"You're not a swimming instructor. I mean, what makes you think you can do this?"

He raises an eyebrow, watching me with that cocky bastard expression. "I was a professional water polo player once. Swimming well is a basic requirement."

"That doesn't mean you can teach me," I say sulkily. He chuckles and it's so distracting.

"Believe me. I can handle you." He stares straight at me and my breath catches. There is a double meaning in those words and the challenge sends a rush of adrenaline through my blood. In other circumstances, I would not even entertain the idea of interacting with someone I find so attractive. Marc is the only man I'm interested in, but frankly, I'm desperate and this guy is throwing me a lifeline.

"I'll pay you." *Yes*. This will make me feel better. Just swimming lessons. He laughs.

"No. I'm doing this as a friend."

I narrow my eyes. "We're not friends, Jake."

He laughs again.

"This isn't going to get you anywhere," I say.

He laughs harder this time. "Abrasive, aren't we? Listen, as charming as you are at the moment, I'm not looking to get laid, if that's what you're implying."

I blush scarlet, pinned under his intense gaze. *Dammit*. He's right. What the hell makes me think he'd be interested in me anyway? That was pretty assuming. But there's something in the way he looks at me, though. It takes my breath away. Maybe it's all in my head.

"Well?" he says.

"Okay." *Can I do this?* "I mean, thank you. If you think you want to help me, that would be great."

"Right on. We can start tomorrow. What time are you free?"

"Um, I'm working the lunch shift. Ten to two."

"We can work before and after. I'll meet you here at seven."

Shit. That's early. "Okay," I mutter. He's so bossy. I'm already questioning whether this is a good idea. But what choice do I have?

He leans closer and I hold my breath. His eyes lock into mine and I'm lost once again in the kaleidoscope of shades inside them.

"You can do this, Natalia. You can." He smiles and slides out of the jacuzzi with impressive grace. I don't exhale until he's a good distance away. His voice saying my name is echoing in my head, and I already know this will be a challenge in more than one way.

Chapter 8: *Jake*

I close the door to my room and walk to the window, raking both hands through my hair. What the fuck did I just commit to? That was stupid, not to mention expensive. But the thought of spending the next two days with Natalia instantly washes off my irritation. Isn't this what I was after?

I unpack my duffel bag and sink in the bed, glad Tamara is gone and I have the space to myself. I scan through my email and there's a response from my contractor telling me he will add the modifications and we should be hearing about the permits this week. Good. As soon as I get confirmation, I can wire the down payment for the lot. The owner already accepted my offer and has agreed to give me a few more days until the permits clear. Everything is on track and if there are no more hurdles we'll break ground in Cardiff as soon as mid-March.

On my phone screen there's a text message from Tamara saying she had a great time and asking me if I'm available again in a couple of weeks. I need to politely reinforce that our relationship is a business transaction so she doesn't get the wrong idea. I've had clients get a bit too needy before and it never ends well. I text her a quick response letting her know it was good to see her, as always, but I'll be busy for the next month. There are several more texts from other clients. But as I read through them, a thick sense of dread fills me. I usually don't give in to feelings that pull me down. I'm content with the lifestyle I've chosen and have done more than well. I have enough money put away for the surf shop and will probably keep a few clients after that. Maintaining casual relationships with women is easy, and as long as they don't expect to reel me in deeper, it works just fine. An image of Natalia's eyes welled with tears flashes through my thoughts and the dread resurfaces. Those fierce green eyes are full of secrets. *So are yours.* I wonder what she would think of my occupation. Women always look at me differently when I tell them. They want to be appalled, but they can't help being intrigued. They want to know if I'm worth every penny in bed. Part of me wants to tell Natalia, just to watch her reaction. Better hold off on that for now.

The following morning, the pool area is deserted. Not much interest from the other guests in swimming at seven a.m. in the middle of winter. My breath morphs into steam as I approach the foggy surface of the pool. Natalia is already waiting by the edge, her feet swirling underwater on the first step as she hugs a thick robe around her. Her face lights up when she sees me.

"Hey." She smiles and it goes straight to the pit of my stomach.

"Hey." I smile back. "Ready?"

She shrugs and gives me a small nod of resignation.

"We don't have a lot of time," I say. "But let's start slow. The first thing is to get you to feel comfortable when you're in the water."

"Piece of cake." She smirks. I tilt my head to the side and she blinks, then raises her palms up.

"Okay. Sorry. You were saying?"

"Right. I want you to hold my hands and step in. Slow." I see the immediate change in her expression. The humor is gone and she blanches. "It's okay," I reassure her. "I've got you." I wait until she rids herself of her robe, and as she does, I can't help taking in the soft curves of her body. She's fucking perfect everywhere in a black one piece that does excellent things for her cleavage. I don't want to look like a perv, so I keep my eyes on hers. She's frowning, and as she looks at the water she bites her lip hard. I tug on her chin to release it and she stills at the contact. "Relax." I shrug off my robe and take her hands. She squeezes mine so tight I'm wondering if I'll ever be able to use them again. I smile. "You have a very firm grip."

She gasps. "Sorry." Her face is grim and I wish I could pull her into my arms.

"It's okay. Just one step at a time."

She takes a hesitant first step into the pool. Her breathing is shallow, and I can see how difficult this is for her. She wasn't kidding when she said she doubted she could do this. Obviously what happened to her when she was young had great impact. I try to recall my training as a lifeguard when it came to dealing with people that are drowning. Their first instinct is to clutch their arms around your neck in panic, which doesn't allow either one of you to swim. I can see that same panic in her eyes. I need to get her to relax. It takes her forever to advance another step. At this rate, we'll be here until tomorrow, and despite the warm water, it's fucking freezing.

"Natalia," I say softly, but in a firm tone. "Look at me." She looks up with wide eyes. "Keep walking until you're all the way into the water. I will not let go of you. This is not that different from the jacuzzi." I smile. She looks terrified, but nods.

"Okay," she whispers. Her chest is heaving in rapid, short breaths. I keep my eyes on hers. She takes slow steps, and I tug her hands gently farther into the water. It takes an eternity for her to be all the way in. She squeezes her eyes shut as I slowly lure her toward the deep end.

"Stop. Please stop. I need a sec." Her voice is hoarse and I can tell she's making a huge effort. I give her a few moments to get used to being all the way into the water. It is up to her chest now. Her hands are crushing mine.

"Natalia. Open your eyes."

She shakes her head no.

"I promise it's okay. I won't let go."

She opens one eye and I smile, then she opens the other and swallows when she realizes how far in we are. "Shit."

"You made it this far, and you're okay." I smile.

"I'm not okay," she pants. "I am flipping out, Jake. Please don't let go." She squeezes my hands tighter. Out of the corner of my eye, I see a figure approaching the pool. A guy in a robe and swim cap. I've seen him swimming laps here before. Her back is turned, so she doesn't see him. She follows my gaze and her eyes widen. "What?"

"Nothing. Just another swimmer. You're good."

She lets a shallow breath out and her eyes stay on mine. She's afraid to look away, I can tell. The swimmer leaps into the water with a loud splash, startling her. Before I can blink she's in my arms, gripping my neck in a deadlock, her eyes squeezed shut. My arms instinctively wrap around her and I'm struck by the scent of fresh jasmine coming from her hair, which is loosely tied in a ponytail. *Fuck.* My dick is immediately aware of her body pressed so tight against mine. She's breathing hard, and I slowly ease her toward the steps again.

"You're okay. It's just another swimmer. See?" I coerce her to open her eyes. She does and relaxes a fraction, nodding.

"Right." She breathes in and out. "I am sorry, Jake. Maybe this was not a good idea."

I can tell she's embarrassed. I hold her face in my hand and her eyes dart to my mouth. *Christ.* I lift her chin up a little so our eyes meet. "You're doing great. It takes time, but look at how far you've come. This is only the first lesson." I smile. And I mean it. I'm so impressed at how brave she's been. I can see how difficult this is for her, and yet, she's still willing to try. It makes me want to see her succeed even more.

"Come on. We can take a break and try again." She looks relieved as I say this. When we reach the shallow end, she lets go. My body protests at the distance with hers. Having her wrapped in my arms felt a lot better than I'm willing to admit.

Our second attempt is a little easier. She lets me lure her in all the way to her shoulders. She's still tense, but seems a bit more at ease and it gives me hope. On our third attempt, I hold her body up parallel to the surface so she's almost floating. It takes a few tries, but she starts to relax. I think she trusts me a little more and that helps. I sway her back and forth gently and tell her to let go. It is not easy, but she's trying. She really wants this to work. With her eyes closed and her hair fanned out into the water, she looks like a mermaid. Her hair tie is lost somewhere, but she doesn't seem to have noticed and I'm liking the sight of her hair swaying in the water way too much, so I stay quiet. As I get distracted water trickles in through her half-parted lips and she jerks up, coughing. Her arms are death-gripping my neck again and I laugh. She asks me if we can take a break. She looks drained from the tension, and she also has to get ready for her shift. I reassure her she has done great and tell her I'm proud. She smirks, but she knows she's done well.

"I'll meet you here again this afternoon?" I smile. I'm invaded by a sudden sense of hollowness for having to say goodbye to her. "What time?"

She thinks for a moment. "Um, I'm done at two. So maybe four? Or later if you're busy."

"Four works. I have a few things to do and it'll give me enough time to hit the slopes."

She smiles, looking genuinely pleased. "Thank you, Jake." And it fills my chest completely.

"You're welcome. You did well." I nod, leaning on the edge as she goes. Then I reach for my goggles and sprint into a butterfly stroke to rid my body of the sudden exhilaration that surges through me.

Chapter 9: *Natalia*:

Dani and Zack have already set up our station when I barge into the lounge. Zack raises his eyebrows. I'm never late. Dani gives me a wicked grin and nods.

"You look a bit ruffled up. Was he good?" She winks.

I ignore her and pull my hair up in a ponytail, catching my breath. "I'm pooped. Who knew learning how to swim could be this exhausting."

"Well." Dani chuckles. "You were probably distracted by your instructor's yummy looks. How did you get the hottest guy in the lodge to give you private swimming lessons?"

"I did not *get* him to do anything. He offered." I frown.

"Right. Lucky you." She laughs. Zack shakes his head and says nothing. I *am* lucky last night resulted in big winnings for both of us, so I'm hoping he'll give me a pass for being late.

The lounge is packed with the morning skiers. Even though it's only Wednesday, the lodge is filling up quickly with the weekend crowd. This means good tips, so everyone's mood is up. Dani and I attend to our respective stations. As we wait for Zack to fill our drink orders, she quizzes me about my morning lesson with Jake. I keep it vague, but she's relentless and tries to make everything I say sound dirty.

"I told you. It's not like that. He's just...really nice. Will you give that rotten brain of yours a break?"

She gives me a smug smile. "If you don't want him, I'll take him. Would that be weird?" She scrunches her nose. "I can get over it, if you can."

"*Dani*." I sigh. "Just...stop, okay?" I whip around and storm to my section, doing my best to ignore her grilling the rest of our shift.

Jake is already waiting when I hurry out to the pool. As I approach, I frown at the three swimmers occupying the lanes. Jake catches the change in my expression and laughs, shaking his head. The jacuzzi is also taken by two girls that look tipsy and frankly, are being way too loud. They are giggling at two guys that are sitting on the edge with their feet in the water and the rest of their ski clothes still on.

"I thought you bailed on me." Jake greets me with a genuine smile that makes me feel instantly warm. I don't even want to admit to myself how much I've been looking forward to our session. I made several mistakes in my orders at lunch because I was too distracted thinking about the way Jake was holding me in the water this morning. It was as if a swarm of butterflies had invaded me, their wings thrumming frantically inside my stomach. Then that *other* dream last night...After the horrid nightmares where Tango saves me from drowning over and over, I had this erotic dream about Jake. My mouth is dry as flashbacks cross through my mind, unbidden. Jake pressing me against the jacuzzi wall, our faces covered in sweat as he grips my hair at the nape and his tongue thrusts into my mouth.

"Hey." He smiles and I blush furiously.

"Sorry. My shift ran long."

"You okay? You look a bit tired."

I pull my hair up in a knot. "I'm fine. Just had a late poker game last night." I look up at him. "It was a favor I owed Zack, before you say anything. Then I had nightmares the rest of the night."

He frowns. "Nightmares?"

"Yes. About the water." I keep the other dream to myself.

"Do you want to tell me?" He looks concerned and it's endearing.

"No." I shake my head. "I don't want to think about it. Let's get started."

"Okay." He nods, eyeing me warily. "How do you feel about the progress we've made so far?"

I smile. "I'm not going to lie. It still makes me very, very nervous to get into the pool, but the panic is much less."

"Okay," he says, and I think he's pleased with my response. "Today I'm going to teach you to *not* drown."

"Helpful." I nod and he chuckles.

"I'm glad your sarcasm is intact. Get in the water."

I stifle a smile at his bossy tone, and obey. Anxiety expands in my chest with every step. He watches me patiently until the water is up to my waist and I glance up, letting him know this is as far as I'm willing to go. He pulls his robe off and I look away because I don't want to stare at him in that speedo. It's amazing how someone like Jake can make a skimpy scrap of fabric look so...hot.

He quickly gets into the water and reaches for something on the edge of the pool.

"Here. Put these on." He hands me a pair of goggles and I raise my eyebrows. *No way.* He shakes his head. "Just put them on. I want you to be able to see my legs under water. I'm going to teach you how to egg-beat."

"Egg *what?*"

"You'll learn the egg-beater movement. It's what water polo players do to stay above water. Treading."

I eye him skeptically and slip the goggles on. He takes me deeper into the pool until the water is up to my shoulders. He's much taller than me, about six feet four, I guess, so he has to go in deeper than me. Then he moves a bit farther and instructs me to dip my face in the water and just watch his legs. This morning he made me put my head all the way underwater several times. I hated it at first and needed him to hold my hand, but I want to show him he isn't wasting his time, so even though my heart is kicking the hell out of my chest, I push myself and do it on my own. Underwater, he's swirling his lower legs at the knees in a movement that resembles the whisks of a hand mixer. Exactly like he described. It looks like he's egg-beating with his legs. I come up for air, then dip my face in and watch him again. While he does this, his hands go up and down in a flying-like movement that allows him to keep his head and even his shoulders above water. My attention is temporarily derailed by the way his muscles flex underwater. I watch him for a long while, knowing he can't see me. It's beautiful. I scold myself and come up for air. I'm impressed because above the surface, he's almost immobile.

"Now you try," he says. I feel the panic rise and I think he sees it on my face because he holds my forearms as I try the movement he just explained. It takes me several attempts. My legs are not cooperating and the fact that our bodies are so close is a major distraction. I try to focus and not gape at the work of art that are his arms and shoulders. Every single muscle is outlined as if someone just Photoshopped him for a swimsuit ad. His hair is wet, and beads of water trickle down his forehead. Steam rises from the pool surface, giving him this god-like aura.

He's *very* distracting.

I frown and coerce my mind to concentrate, and finally I think I get it, because he slowly slides his hands down my arms until he's holding only my fingers. I'm ecstatic and want to scream that I did it, but I don't want to let go of him. He then holds only one of my hands and tells me to do the flying movement with the other. When he thinks I've got it, he tells me he's going to let go. I look at him with wide eyes and he smiles.

"You can do it, Natalia." The way he says my name causes me to lose my coordination and I panic, whipping my limbs in every direction, splashing him as I flap my arms and gasp for air. He immediately wraps his arms around me and tells me it's okay.

"You did great," he says into my ear, and a surge of electricity travels through me. I'm holding on to his neck for my life, panting, but the soothing tone of his voice relaxes me, and I slowly loosen my grip. The group at the jacuzzi is staring in our direction, and the girls are laughing out loud. I scowl at them and want to tell them to fuck off.

"They're just some stupid drunks. Don't worry about them," he says, and I have to fight the urge to kiss him. Nobody has made me feel this safe in years. Not even Marc. Marc is attentive, but patience is not his strong suit. I can't imagine him doing what Jake is doing for me right now. The only person that made me feel something close to this was...Tango, an eternity ago.

I shake off the thought and look up at Jake. He's watching me with those warm eyes that remind me of the way cognac feels as it slides down your throat on a cold day. *Shit*. I push away my day fantasy with this almost stranger and offer him a small, apologetic smile.

"Should we try again?" I say, and I think he's pleased because his answering smile is dazzling. In an effort to break the spell from that smile, I try to think of Marc, but I really don't want to think of Marc right now. Jake's presence is so strong there's no room for anything else. So I go with it.

By the end of the lesson, I've got the egg-beater thing down and Jake praises me for my progress.

"Wanna have a drink? You've earned it."

I look up at the lodge. Fraternizing with the guests is not encouraged and I'm already pushing my luck with the swimming lessons. The only reason I got away with it was because Sarah, our manager, likes me and thinks I'm her pet project, so she was eager to help.

"Natalia, it's just a drink. Not a proposition. But it's cool if you don't feel like it." He smiles.

"It's not that. This place likes gossip, and I'm already bending the rules with the lessons."

He laughs. "We can go into town. I wouldn't mind having my last dinner out."

My breath catches when he says that, reminding me this will be his last night here. I can't help the feeling of emptiness that washes over me, and I already know I want to have more time with him. I know it's wrong, but I tell myself we are just friends and he's not interested in me in a romantic way. I'm a pretty lousy liar.

I tell him I prefer to take a cab, and we make arrangements to meet at a restaurant downtown. Drinks just turned into dinner.

In my room, I try on every outfit I brought, which adds up to a grand total of five. Nothing seems right. I sigh out loud.

Dani storms in from the gym and takes in the mess of clothes on my bed. "Hot date?"

"I'm meeting Jake for a drink. It's *not* a date."

She rolls her eyes. "Right."

"*Dani*," I snap.

She raises her palms up. "Hey, I'm not judging. You need to venture out and that's a good thing."

"Why don't you like Marc? You're always telling me to venture out. I'm not going to cheat on him."

"It's not that I don't like him. I'm just not as convinced as you are that he's the right match for you."

"*Why?*" I whip around.

"I don't know." She plops down on the bed. "Too self-absorbed, I guess. I actually think he loves himself more than he loves you. Sorry." She shrugs. "I get the money thing and all that, but I'm not sold on the guy. I don't trust him doing the long distance thing, either. He seems way too cool about it."

"Dani. Marc would *never* cheat on me. Jesus. And you know I'm not with him because he has money. Can you give it a rest? I'm going to marry him and I don't want things between you and me to be weird."

"Fine. I've said my peace. I'm letting you be. But let yourself have a good time. That hot guy out there is doing way more than is required for a *friend* and I think you deserve some of that. Let loose."

"Dani, please just help me find something to wear and shut up."

She chuckles as she stands up, then opens her closet and pulls out a short black dress with long sleeves and a square neck. It's very sexy and the material looks incredibly soft.

"Here." She hands me the dress. "I haven't worn it yet, but it will look good on you."

I grin, because it's perfect. "Really?"

"Really." She grins back.

Twenty minutes later, I'm showered, dressed in the black short dress, and pulling my black knee-high boots on. I slip into a red coat that goes down to my knees and I'm rushing to the door where my taxi is waiting. And I can't remember the last time I was this excited.

Chapter 10: *Jake*

I am getting dressed for this date wondering what the hell I'm really getting dressed for. This crazy obsession over Natalia has now turned into a wild goose chase. I was expecting that at some point during the last two days, I would find in her what I have been looking for from the start: confirmation that she's no different from all the other women I've ever met. I guess in my head, extending my vacation by two days was not a big deal if in return I got her out of my mind and regained full control of my thoughts.

Epic failure so far.

There hasn't been one moment in the time we've spent together when I didn't want to crush her mouth into a kiss. It's a fucking inconvenience, because the whole time my thoughts have been at war with my dick. Thank God for the pool in winter.

I pull a gray sweater over my head. Black jeans and boots will do. Then grab my leather jacket as I walk out, raking a hand through my hair so it doesn't look like I'm trying hard. I want tonight to be the same as the last two days have been. At some point, Natalia let down her guard and she seems more relaxed around me. I like seeing her that way.

I get into a taxi at the front of the hotel, thinking how ridiculous it is that we're not sharing a ride, but as an employee, appearances matter to Natalia. I wonder what her friends make of the time she's been spending with me. I also wonder if she's told her fiancé she has a new swimming instructor. *Yeah, one that does what you do for a living.* I shake my head. I've never given a fuck about appearances, and I'm not about to start now. Tonight, I'm going to prove to myself she's just like the others. I know I'm a prick for setting her up like this, but I also know it's the only way I'll find peace of mind.

I enter the restaurant and scan the room. The hostess takes her time to appraise me, and stifles a smile while she locates my reservation.

"Jake Harper?" She looks up and her eyes darken. I refrain from rolling mine and nod a response. She swings her hips around her station, makes sure I get a good shot of her ass as she picks up the menus, then glances once over her shoulder.

"Right this way, please."

I follow her to the table I've requested. It is by a floor to ceiling window overlooking the mountain. I've been here with Tamara before. I'm browsing over the wine list when Natalia appears at my side. I stand, and before I can say anything, she tilts her face up and greets me with a kiss on the cheek. I'm momentarily stunned, enjoying the sudden contact with her chilled cheek. She realizes she caught me off guard, and a slight blush raises to her face.

"It's an Argentinean thing," she explains. "The kissing on the cheek. I keep forgetting you guys don't do that here. It's weird to me to shake someone's hand." She smiles as I help her with her coat.

"I don't mind." I shrug, and her smile widens. She looks radiant. Those piercing green eyes are bright and her hair is down in long, raven layers. I haven't seen her hair down since the poker night, and it's definitely my new favorite.

"This place is incredible. Look at that view," she says as I pull out her chair, then gives me a thankful smile.

"Do you come into town much?" I say, drinking in her fresh expression. I haven't seen her this relaxed since…I've never seen her this relaxed.

"Not usually," she says. "Unless it's someone's birthday and we can work out the time off. Most nights I'm dead tired after work. We just stay in and play poker."

"Which is quite profitable in your case." I smile and that slight blush raises to her face again. I need to find more things to make her blush, because it's sort of addicting. Her guard is down and she looks beautiful. She shakes her head.

"Gotta do what you can."

"Indeed. I nod." My eyes are locked on hers and she glances down at the menu, blushing again, and I can't help the shit-eating grin on my face.

I order a bottle of wine and she lifts up the napkin on the bread basket and picks up a bread roll. She breaks a piece and bites into it, making an appreciative sound. I like that she's not hiding the fact that she's hungry. I cannot remember the last time I saw a woman grab a piece of plain white bread and put it in her mouth.

The waiter comes back with the wine and we order our meals. Once again I'm surprised when she orders the Fettuccine and Fungi special and not a skimpy salad like Tamara would have.

We fall into easy conversation, and she tells me about her life in Buenos Aires. I'm fascinated, and want to know every detail. Life in South America sounds fun, careless, and much less regulated than here in every way. I make a mental note to add Buenos Aires to my bucket list.

"So Jake." She smiles. "I usually don't ask people this, but given the fact that we just spent the last two days together and now you know more about my life and aspirations than most people, I'm gonna ask." She sighs.

"What?"

"What do you do for a living?"

And there it is.

I hold her gaze for a moment, pondering. But it's too soon and I'm enjoying having her here, unaffected and unguarded. I'm not ready to give that up, yet.

"Well?" She raises her eyebrows.

"I have plans to open a surf shop. If everything goes well, we will open by mid-March."

Her face lights up. "Really? Where?"

I tilt my head and she blushes. Why does she blush when I tilt my head? "San Diego."

"You're kidding." Her eyes widen and she's watching me as if she's waiting for me to tell her it's a joke.

"Nope. Cardiff, actually. I have friends there that I visit every summer. I've been toying with the idea of having my own shop for a while, and I've always been kind of obsessed with surfboards. So it's finally happening."

"That's...great. I mean…" She shakes her head.

"What? What did you think I was going to say?"

She looks up and suddenly seems embarrassed. "I don't know. I figured you were one of those guys that play golf and live a work-free life. I don't know what pro athletes do when they retire."

I laugh. "My career was not as long as I wished, and water polo athletes are not like football players."

"Why did you stop playing?"

"Shoulder injury," I say. "I pushed it too hard during the Olympics. I was young and thought my body could take anything. That was my last trip."

Her eyebrows shoot up. "You played in the *Olympics*?"

I nod. "Gold medal."

"No way."

I shrug in response. She looks at me for a long moment with a puzzled look of admiration. It's better than being pinned as some has-been living on the products of his glory days.

Our dinner comes and I'm relieved with the change of subject. I smile when she tells me she's starving, and appraises the food on her plate. She grins as she takes a bite, and the way her mouth wraps around her fork sends an instant shot to my groin. It makes me shift on my seat. I smile again because I love that she loves food.

"So what do you do now?" she says, reaching for her glass. "I mean, how do you make a living if you're...retired?"

Ah.

"That's a lot of questions." I smile, because I'm still not ready to answer that. Not until I find out what I want to know about her. "I'm kind of shy." I tilt my head and she stops chewing, then reaches for her wine again. *Yes. I need to tilt my head more.*

She takes a sip and smiles. "You are *not* shy, Jake."

"Okay." I shrug. "You're right. Maybe shy is not the right word. I'm a very private person, though."

She pouts and I have to look away. "Well," she says. "You know a lot about me. I feel at a disadvantage. So you have to tell me."

I laugh. "Very persistent. But seriously, enough about me."

She shakes her head and I'm safe for the moment. We ease into safer territory as she tells me about working at the lodge. It sounds like a fun deal, and she says she makes a lot in tips. I have no doubt. After watching her play poker, I'm sure she does very well for herself.

When we are done with our meal, I order a lemon mousse to share. She smiles. I don't really want dessert, but watching her lips wrap around the spoon as she eats has become my new favorite show. Out of the corner of my eye, I see a small dance floor by a wall of windows and inspiration hits me. The window is now a black screen peppered with the glinting lights from the surrounding homes. In a corner next to the dance floor, a guy sitting on a barstool strums the chords of an acoustic guitar as he hums a slow melody.

"Want to dance?" I say, appraising her reaction. She looks up and her eyes widen. She's conflicted.

"Um, I'm not a great dancer."

Good save. I smile. "Doesn't matter. I am. I'll guide you. Besides, this is a very slow song."

She looks down at her hands before meeting my eyes again. "Jake, I don't know if that's a good idea. I mean, I'm with...someone. I don't think he'd like it if he knew I was slow dancing with another guy." I'm stunned by her loyalty. It's like she just swung a right hook to my jaw. Now I really want to know.

"I promise I won't push the boundaries. I just want to dance with you, Natalia."

She closes her eyes for a moment, and I think I've won.

"Okay. Just one song."

I smile and take her hand as I stand, leading her to the dance floor. I know I'm being a prick. This girl is off the market. My rules about women that are unavailable are also clear: Keep Out. But I have to convince myself Natalia is no different than the other women I've met, and if she's tempted far enough, she will cave. Women can't help lying. They all do it. It's in their DNA. In the end, loyalty means nothing to them.

My arms wrap around her waist while she hesitantly circles hers around my neck. The immediate sensation that fires through me leaves me winded. The scent of jasmine invades me. I close my eyes, and squeeze her a little tighter so I can bury my nose in her hair. She stills and lets out a small gasp. *God.* She's fucking heaven. Her body fits perfectly in my arms, and her warmth feels so incredibly good it's almost unbearable. I have to end this soon. *Just get through with it and walk away, Jake.* My lips brush her neck slightly, almost without touching her. Her skin is soft and I imagine kissing every inch of it, the way I've been imagining her in my bed since we first met. I brush her hair over her other shoulder so I can have full access to her neck. I graze her skin with my lips again, and a shiver runs through her, leaving goose bumps on her neck. My other hand presses against the small of her back, bringing her closer. The fabric of her dress is soft, and I imagine sliding it over her head, slowly peeling it off to reveal the rest of her perfect skin. I squeeze my arms around her and I'm already hard.

"Jake," she whispers, and it's almost inaudible. "I...can't." Her breaths are shallow, and I know she's feeling this as much as I am.

I close my eyes, feeling every inch the asshole that I am, and decide to go for the kill. I thread my fingers in her hair, cradling her face in my hands, and deliberately look at her mouth before meeting her eyes. She looks vulnerable, and I know perfectly well the effect I'm having on her. I have seen it a hundred times before with the others. Her eyes are dark, her lips parted as she breathes in broken breaths, waiting for my next move. I bring her mouth to mine, and just as our lips are about to touch, she shakes her head and presses her hands to my chest.

My heart constricts.

Dread fills me.

"I'm sorry," she whispers. "I really can't. I have to go." Before I can answer she's dashing back to the table. I catch up with her as she's shrugging on her coat. She looks shaken and my mood sinks deeper. *Well done, Jake. You sick douche.* I reach for her hand and wrap mine around it. She doesn't pull it away, but doesn't make eye contact either. She just stares at my hand over hers.

"I'm sorry. I got carried away. Please don't leave," I say, hoping she won't realize the full extent of my assholeness, and maybe I'll have a shot in hell that she'll reconsider. She shakes her head.

"It's fine. It's just…" she sighs. "I shouldn't be here."

I squeeze her hand under mine. "Natalia. You didn't do anything wrong. I'm a dick. I knew where the boundaries were. I promise it won't happen again. Will you stay?"

"Jake—"

"Look. I don't want things to end like this. I enjoyed the time we've spent together. Let's have a coffee, then we'll go."

She looks up and eyes me for a moment, assessing my sincerity, I think.

"Okay," she mutters. And suddenly I can breathe again.

I order two espressos and get the check so we can go whenever she wants. Hoping to ease the weirdness between us, I give her a few pointers for her swimming training so she can practice while I'm gone. When I tell her we should make plans to meet in four days when I come back for my guy's ski trip, she looks down at her hands.

"I don't know Jake. I mean, you've helped me so much, but I don't think it's a good idea."

"Why? Because of what happened tonight?"

She nods. I close my eyes, and let her sincerity slice me open.

"Natalia. In the last couple of days, I've felt something. A guy can hope." I smile.

Asshole. She should punch me.

But she doesn't. She just looks up at me and her eyes are full of regret. It makes me want to crush her into a kiss.

"That's just it," she murmurs. "It's wrong. I love Marc. Besides," she says, looking straight at me with a harder expression, "two days ago, you were here with another woman. Doesn't that mean anything to you?"

This again.

I run both hands through my hair. "I told you. Tamara and I are not in a relationship."

"She was all over you, Jake. How can you just turn that off and switch to someone different?" She looks mad.

"Because she and I have an arrangement."

She frowns. "What kind of arrangement?"

Shit. I let out a heavy sigh. *Fuck it.*

"Tamara is a client."

"What?"

"We see each other every two or three weeks. We go on trips like this, parties, dinners, or just hang out. She doesn't want a relationship and neither do I."

She frowns and is looking at me as if I'm suddenly someone different. "You said *client*."

I nod.

"Are you…"

I nod again.

"*Jesus*. Is that even legal?" She's embarrassed. I couldn't have made things more uncomfortable for her if I'd tried.

"Natalia," I say, and her eyes immediately meet mine. Every time I say her name she reacts this way, like she can't help it. I like that. I like it way too much. She shakes her head as if she's trying to rid herself of my spell.

"How can you do that? I can't even imagine being with someone I don't care about."

"It's a matter of perspective. I do care about Tamara. I just don't want a relationship, and neither does she. It is a consensual agreement between two people that know exactly what they want. No false promises, no unmet expectations. It's simple. It works for me and it makes her happy."

She shakes her head again. She's trying to figure this out.

"Natalia. I'm no different than any other single man. I date who I want. I just don't make bullshit promises that I won't fulfill."

She narrows her eyes. "You get *paid* to have sex with them. That is *not* normal." She's whispering, but her eyes are blazing. Her sudden anger surprises me and in a much deeper level, I think I like the fact that she's angry.

"Like I said." I shrug. "It's a matter of perspective. I'm not taking advantage of anyone. At the end of the day everybody is happy."

She watches me for a long moment. I can almost see the wheels turning in her head. I smile and she tries to scowl. She's mad, but I just made her smile.

"It's not funny. I want to be mad at you, Jake."

I laugh. "Why?"

"You're insanely good-looking. You don't need to do that."

I grin. "Insanely good-looking, huh?"

She blushes scarlet, and it's hard to resist.

"I get exactly what I want, Natalia."

"Everyone wants to love and be loved. You can't say you're above that."

"I'm not compromising my values. Stop trying to rationalize it."

"How many clients do you have?"

I arch an eyebrow. "Curious, aren't we?"

She shrugs, but she's pouting.

"Three at the moment. Usually no more than four."

"And you can make a living? You must be *good*." She frowns and I laugh out loud. She realizes what she's just said and blushes crimson. She's adorable.

"Nobody's ever asked for their money back." I grin and her blush deepens. "So now that you find me appalling and I'm no threat to your engaged status, will you agree to meet again for our next swimming lesson?"

She looks out at the glimmering lights of the mountain, as if the answer is waiting out there somewhere, then meets my eyes.

"I don't find you appalling, Jake. I just...I don't understand. But whatever. I'm not judging. I can't hang out with you like this anymore. I'm engaged. It feels wrong. Like cheating...It's better if we leave things as they are."

Once again, her sincerity floors me. Despite what she says, I'm sure she's repelled by my confession. Yet, I can tell she felt something for me. *Fuck, Jake. Way to make a mess of things.* The sudden need to see her again fills me. I have to find a way. Right now I'm losing her.

I rack my brain for something useful. She's proved me wrong in every way possible and that makes the pull that lures me to her so much stronger. I know I have no right, and yet, I can't let go.

"Shall we?" she says, and I'm free falling. No lifeline.

I stand up and we walk out.

Outside, the valet signals to a taxi parked a few feet away.

"Can we ride together?" I ask.

She glances at her watch. "Sure. It's late. I think I'm safe from the paparazzi."

On the car ride, she's quiet. I scramble for something to say, an excuse to see her again, but come up empty. At least I know she'll be here when I come back in a few days, but I'll be sharing a villa with two other guys, and it will be harder to get time alone with her.

When we get back to the lodge, it's after midnight. I walk her to the employee entrance, now deserted. The runs are closed. On the mountain, faint lights illuminate the chairlift, casting a ghostly glow over the snow. She shivers in her coat, her breath coming out in swirls of vapor.

I want to hug her.

"So...I guess I'll see you." She smiles, but it doesn't reach her eyes.

I'm desperate.

I'm falling.

She turns to leave, but I pull her in and envelope her in my arms. She takes in a sharp breath, but doesn't push me away. Hope explodes inside me like the fourth of July.

"It was really, really nice meeting you, Natalia. I'll be back here in four days. We can finish our lessons then."

"Jake…" she whispers. Her eyes are closed.

"You take care." I press a kiss on her forehead, then turn around, feeling half of me is still where she's standing.

Chapter 11: *Natalia*:

I'm lying on my back, sprawled out naked on Jake's bed.

What am I doing on Jake's bed?

From the other side of the room, he saunters toward me. He, too, is gloriously naked. I bite my lip in appreciation. God, he's beautiful. In the dim light of the moon, every one of his muscles is outlined. He stands at the foot of the bed, drinking me in. My heart is beating so fast, I have to close my eyes for a second and remind myself to take a breath.

"You're beautiful," he says, and I smile because that's exactly what I'm thinking about him at the moment.

"Come here, Jake." My voice is laced with want.

A winning smile stretches on his face as he lowers himself to me. He kisses me, slowly, and it's so bewitching I can't concentrate on anything but that perfect mouth molding to mine. His lips move to my jaw, and down to my neck, his tongue exploring every inch of me with sensual precision, torturing me. He continues his journey south and I squirm. He smiles against my stomach, but doesn't stop. Fire flares inside me, and I clench the sheet at my sides. His hands rake my thighs, caressing me with the tips of his fingers. He then grips my legs at the knees and spreads them farther apart. *Damn.* I gasp as his tongue slips between my legs.

"Jake," I cry. But he's relentless. His expert tongue slides in and out of me, torturing me, driving me insane. *God*, is it possible to feel this much? He doesn't stop, and I'm already climbing, panting, clutching his hair as I moan a pleading. He then slips his fingers inside me, swirling them as his tongue pushes me beyond anything I've ever experienced.

And I'm lost.

I come like a freight train, screaming his name. He's immediately on top of me and thrusts inside me before I can take a breath. His mouth smothers mine, and he starts to move. *God.* He fills me completely as he rocks in and out of me. I'm in ecstasy. The way he moves is inebriating, and even though I'm spent, I completely surrender. It's heaven and hell all at once. My body is exhausted and yet, I want more.

I want all of him.

I start to climb again and he groans in appreciation. The sound ripples through me and I clench my hands in his hair, pressing myself against him. He moves faster, faster, and I start tightening again. *Jesus.*

"That's right, baby. Let go." His low, hoarse voice is my undoing and I explode around him, weightless. Free.

There's nothing else.

Just Jake.

He rolls onto his back. We are both panting. Sweat and sex in the air. It's intoxicating, and I smile because I've never been happier.

He then turns on his side, propping up on his elbow. He's smiling at me. I'm smiling at him.

"That will be two thousand dollars," he says.

I wake up with a jolt.

What the hell?

I look around the room, disoriented. I'm breathing hard and my tank top is drenched in sweat. *Jesus.* I'm still trembling with the aftershocks of my orgasm. I close my eyes and press my forehead to my palm, rubbing off the flashes of the still vivid dream.

When I finally open my eyes, the nightstand clock tells me it's nine in the morning.

Shit.

I have never had a wet dream before, and I'm suddenly embarrassed. Good thing Dani is not here, and Jake's most likely gone by now.

Jake.

A memory of his lips grazing my neck while we were dancing flashes in my mind, sending goose bumps down my arms. I push it away. Dammit. This is a runaway train. I need to see Marc.

I open my laptop, my hands unsteady from the dream, and get on the airline website. Whatever it will cost me, I'm buying a ticket to Los Angeles. I need to see Marc this weekend. The fares are astronomical, but the blood still pulsing behind my ears convinces me it's the right thing to do. If I can get one of the other girls to switch shifts with me, I can leave as soon as tomorrow.

I decide I have a good chance of getting my shift covered, and buy a ticket for tomorrow night. I want to text Marc so he can pick me up at the airport, but then resolve to surprise him. I can take a cab for the 5 mile ride to his home in Manhattan Beach. I know he will be at home all weekend preparing for a presentation. He works way too much. Before pitches he doesn't go out at all, so it's almost a given he will stay in, even though it'll be Friday night when I arrive.

Ten minutes later, I'm booked on the 3:45 pm flight that will get me to LAX by seven in the evening.

I can breathe.

Dani startles me when she barges into the room dressed in workout clothes. She frowns and pulls out one of her earphones.

"What the hell?"

"What?"

"You look...I don't know. Weird. Unhinged. *Wait*." Her eyes widen. "Is it in any way related to last night? OMG tell me right now."

"Dani." I frown. "No. I told you. Last night was just...dinner."

She shakes her head. "I don't believe you. Spit it out."

I get up from the chair and plop back on the bed. "I need to see Marc. I'm going crazy."

"I *knew* it!"

"Dani. Stop. I'm not joking. This sucks. I was happy with everything until I met Jake."

"Do you like him? I mean, who would blame you. He's fucking gorgeous."

I let out a long sigh. "I don't do that, Dani. You know me. I don't check out other guys. There's always been just Marc."

I look up at her and her forehead is creased, but she's biting her tongue. It doesn't matter because I already know what she thinks. She thinks this is good.

"I bought a ticket to Los Angeles for tomorrow."

"You *what*?"

I nod. "I need to see him, Dani. I need Marc to erase all these thoughts I have about Jake."

"So you *do* like him. This is what all this is about. Holy shit. Why didn't you tell me before?"

"I don't know. It's not even really Jake. It's the fact that I allowed myself to be swayed by someone that is not Marc."

"It *is* Jake, Natalia. He's goddamn beautiful."

I shake my head. "No. Jake and I would never work."

"Why?"

"Because. It just wouldn't." I don't want to tell Dani what I know about Jake. She wouldn't tell anyone, but for some reason it feels demeaning toward him.

Dani sighs out loud, and heads to the shower. "Lane will be happy to switch shifts with you," she says from inside the bathroom. "She needs Monday and Tuesday off and Sarah told her to find someone herself. The schedule is packed."

The rest of the day, I'm restless. I work out, pack my bag for tomorrow, and work my shift with Dani and Zack. Lane has agreed to switch shifts with me, and I can't wait until tomorrow. I'm glad Jake has already left and that I didn't run into him. The way he looked at me last night as he said goodbye, still burns in my chest. I need to 'deJake' myself, and Friday can't come soon enough.

It is a little after seven in the evening when I finally get off the plane. I have only a carry-on so that saves me time. At the curb, I hail a taxi and give the driver Marc's address. I shift in my seat with anticipation. I wonder what Marc is doing right now, and how he will react to my impromptu visit. I miss him. A weekend alone with Marc is what I need.

Twenty minutes later, I pay the driver and shoulder my duffel bag. I have never really liked Los Angeles. During the times I visited Marc, I always got that feeling of the morning after the party, cloudy minds foggy with ecstasy and smog. Marc lives in Manhattan Beach, a trendy town that few can afford. I find it a bit too crafted, but I love the beach, so I'm hoping it will grow on me.

I look up at Marc's home on The Strand and smile. The evening is barely cool compared to Aspen, the air deliciously saturated with the salty scent of the ocean and seaweed. My heart kicks my chest and starts beating faster because the lights just went on upstairs.

Drinking in the salted evening air, I stride up the short steps to the front door.

I ring the bell, bouncing on the tips of my toes. The lights go on in the hallway and my pulse sprints. Most of the walls in Marc's multi-million dollar home are paneled with glass, offering an unobstructed view of the ocean from pretty much every corner. The glass by the front door is frosted for privacy, so I can't see him. I smile when I hear footsteps padding closer.

The door swings open, and I'm immediately confused. My smile vanishes, and I frown.

"May I help you?" A Barbie-like chick, with lips that are way too plump to be real, is staring at me with an arched eyebrow. I open my mouth with a dozen scenarios running through my head as to why this half-naked woman is opening the door to my fiancé's home.

"Well?" she whines. Her lips make me think of a butthole and I suddenly want to laugh out loud. Then my smile fades as I take a closer look at her attire. Her legs are bare under the shirt she's wearing that goes down just below her hips.

His shirt.

I know it's his, because I bought it for him at The Who concert last year in L.A.

My eyes slowly travel up, as anger unfolds from within me. I clench my teeth and meet her puzzled expression with a deadly glare. If my eyes were machine guns they'd be firing bullets into her.

"Where's Marc?" I mutter, closing my hands into fists to derail the impulse to clutch them around her over-tanned whore neck.

"Um." She frowns and looks around behind her shoulder.

A second pair of footsteps approaches. This time they belong to Marc.

"Who is it bab—" His sentence is left hanging from his half-open mouth as he stares at me with wide eyes. His face blanches, and it looks like he's forgotten how to breathe.

"Hey, *babe*," I say, glaring at him as the last of the oxygen leaves my body. I feel like I'm going to pass out right here on his doorstep. Or throw up. I hope it's the latter, and that it leaves a huge mess for him to clean.

"Nati," he finally says, and my stomach churns in disgust. I don't want him to say my name.

Ever. Again.

Butt-lips-girl raises her palms and turns around toward the stairs. I narrow my eyes, watching her whore ass take the steps two at a time. *Yeah, you run.*

Marc runs both hands through his hair. He looks lost. Then he opens the door wider so I can come in. But I don't.

I have no intention of going in.

"What the hell, Marc?" I mutter.

"It's not what it looks like," he has the nerve to say. "I mean, it is, but I can explain."

"Explain?" I let out a humorless chuckle.

He exhales a sharp breath. "It doesn't mean anything, Nati. I'm in love with you. This just...*Shit*." He presses his forehead against the edge of the door.

I hate it when guys say that when they get caught cheating. 'It didn't mean anything.' Because it does.

"It means *everything*, Marc. It means you're a cheating, fucking lying son of a bitch. I want nothing to do with you. Ever."

I whip around and rush down the steps to the street. He catches up with me and grips my arm. I yank it off, and give him a murderous glare. He lets go.

"Please, Nati. Please don't go. Let's talk about this."

"I don't want to fucking talk to you. Ever again," I snarl. Tears fill my eyes and spill. My words make him take a step back. He's looking at me with a mix of regret and desperation.

"Please. I don't want you to leave. We can go somewhere else and talk."

"No." I turn around and set off toward the street.

"Nati, please." He's following me, and for the first time, I notice he's wearing boxers under his shirt, and he's barefoot. I hope he steps on a rusted nail. "Will you stop?"

I whip around. "Get the fuck away from me."

"Where are you going?"

"Back to the fucking airport."

"Nati. Please. It's late. Just...wait until tomorrow."

"Fuck you, Marc. I hope you and butt-lips are fucking happy together."

"Goddammit, Nati. Fucking stop for a second so we can have a proper conversation about this." He snatches my elbow and I try to shake him off, but he's gripping me hard.

"Let go," I snap.

"Stop *walking*," he growls.

"What seems to be the problem?" A cop steps out of a deli. He's looking at Marc with a frown. His eyes dart down, taking in his half-dressed appearance, then stop on the hand that is gripping my elbow.

"Everything okay, ma'am?" His eyes are now on me. I look at Marc with flared nostrils and I almost smile. *Fuck you, asshole.*

"No. I need a taxi." I lock eyes with the cop and he nods once, then looks at Marc.

"I sure hope you have somewhere else to be, or you'll get a free ride to the station."

Marc lets go of me and shakes his head. His eyes search mine. "We need to talk."

"I don't need to talk to you. I need a taxi to the airport."

The cop gives Marc a pointed look, and he turns around, looking defeated. I watch his cheating ass retreat, and my throat thickens. I don't want to cry in front of the cop. He'll feel bad and may not want to let me go. Right now, I need to be in a fucking plane that will take me away from Marc and this hollow city with no soul.

"Are you okay? Was that man bothering you?"

I shake my head. "No. I just want to get a taxi, please."

He eyes me warily, and waits until a cab drives by, then hails it. As I slide in, he tells me to take care and I thank him.

Life is laughing at me from above, because there are no departing flights to Aspen until tomorrow morning. I walk to a sitting area, and curl up in a corner, pulling my knees up. I feel numb. Cold from the inside. I vaguely wonder if this is all a nightmare and Dani is about to shake me awake.

I miss Dani and Zack.

My phone rings, and I turn it off when I see Marc's name on the screen. I hope he fucking burns in cheaters' hell.

I close my eyes and think about Jake and how ironic it is that it was I who felt sorry for him. I now realize how much wiser his theory is. If I hadn't put myself out there, if I hadn't trusted Marc, this wouldn't have happened. Tango's voice barges in my thoughts *'You can't outsmart getting hurt, Princess.'* He always called me Princess. I start to cry, pressing my forehead to my knees to force the cutting memory away. I haven't felt this alone since that day. The day I found out Tango had left me alone in this shell of a world. I miss him.

I walk around the airport and fall asleep a couple of times in the waiting areas by the gates, but the seats are rigid and uncomfortable.

By the time my flight boards at five in the morning, I'm exhausted. I turn my phone back on, knowing Marc will most likely be asleep and won't call me. I have a few voicemails and seventeen text messages from him, most of them starting with 'Please' and 'Sorry.' I delete them without reading them. Dani also sent a text asking how my reunion with Marc went. I shake my head. She'll be thrilled when I tell her Marc is a lying cheating prick and she gets to say 'I told you so.'

I'm asleep before we take off, and the last image I see in my head is Jake smiling.

Chapter 12: *Jake*

The bartender at the Cardiff Shack slides me a beer and I raise my glass for a toast with my contractor. All the plans have been approved, and this afternoon the landlord and I signed the rest of the paperwork. The property for the surf shop is now mine. I can't help the grin on my face, and the first thought that comes to my mind is Natalia. I want to tell her. I know she'll be happy for me. I dismiss the thought, and take a long swig of cold beer.

Two hours later, I'm back at Pete's house. He and I became friends when we both made the National team during my water polo days. Pete is married to Sydney, another retired water polo athlete, and they have a baby girl, little Mia. They live in Cardiff, and own a small club in Del Mar, where Pete coaches young athletes. He's asked me to work with him many times. My gold medal is a great marketing tool for his club and I know it would be fun, but my chosen profession as a male escort could be a liability for Pete and I don't want to bring that on him and Sydney. Pete knows what I do, and says he doesn't care, and although I kind of love him for that, I'd rather not put him at risk. He's convinced me to run short clinics now and then, and in exchange, I get to crash at his house whenever I come to San Diego.

"If you move to Cardiff, I'm S.O.L., Jake. Does that mean I'll have to start paying you for the winter clinics?" He laughs.

"No. I have fun doing it. Brings back good memories."

"Yeah, it does." He grins. "Too bad you can't tap into my club for new clients. There are so many divorcées. Pisses Syd off sometimes. They're ruthless." He shakes his head.

I laugh. "You better look out man, that's how I started."

"I wish." He grins. "I'd be making money instead of breaking even. So how's it all going to work out now that you're a *legitimate business owner*?" He smirks.

"I'm actually thinking about retiring."

"Right."

"I'm serious."

He gives me a long look.

"I can't do this forever, Pete. Besides, it's starting to get old. Women get clingy after a while, and I feel like an asshole every time I'm forced to face them with the fact that what we have is nothing more than a business transaction."

Pete whistles through his teeth and shakes his head.

"What?" I frown.

"What's her name?" He watches me like he just figured out my magic trick. Pete is the only person I can talk to openly. He doesn't judge, and has no filter when it comes to giving his opinion, which I like and respect about him. But in this moment I fucking hate that he can see right through me. I hang on to my pride and pretend.

"Whose name?"

He grins and shakes his head. "Wow, Jake. I never thought I'd see the day when a chick grounded you. Tell me her fucking name, man."

I shrug. "Doesn't matter. She's engaged."

"Ouch."

"Yeah." I sigh. "I've never met anyone like her, though. She's fun and witty, but kind of jagged at times. Street smart, too, and you should see her playing poker."

"Shit, dude." He laughs. "This is serious."

I look up at him and realize that, for the first time in my life, I just admitted out loud that I'm genuinely interested in someone. Pete is watching me with amusement, having come to the same realization.

"What are you going to do?" he asks.

I look up and lock eyes with him.

"Fight."

Chapter 13: *Natalia*:

It is midmorning by the time I get back to the lodge. Dani is most likely at the gym, or skiing. I scurry in, keeping my head down as I follow the hallway to my room. It is empty, and I'm relieved. I go to the bathroom to brush my teeth and flinch when I look in the mirror. My eyes are swollen and red rimmed, and there are streaks of dry mascara on my cheeks. *And the Oscar for most pathetic goes to...Natalia Prinz.*

I pull a sweatshirt over my head, then sink into my bed, curling into a ball. Dani wakes me up sometime later when she opens the door to the room and turns the light on.

"Oh, shit. You scared the hell out of me. What are you doing here? I thought you weren't coming back till tomorrow."

I groan.

"What happened," she says in a sharper tone.

I turn around in my bed, and look up at her. She's dressed in gym clothes, her arms crossed over her chest.

"Bad trip," I say.

She erases the distance and sits beside me on the bed. "Tell me. What happened."

I sit up against the headboard, and stare through the window at the snow outside. "A fucking Barbie stuffed with collagen opened Marc's door, wearing only his Roger Daltrey T-shirt."

"Fucking son of a bitch." Dani's eyes narrow as she shakes her head and lets out a sharp breath.

"Yup. That sums it up."

She pulls me into her arms and squeezes me tight. The thickness in my throat swells again.

"I'm sorry, Natalia."

"You were right about him, Dani. Now you get to say you told me so."

"No, Nati. I'm a cynic. That doesn't make me right, just skeptical and untrusting in general. But Marc is a fucking prick." She pulls me at arm's length. "This doesn't change anything for you, right? You're still taking the internship like you planned."

I shrug. "I don't know. Maybe. Right now I really can't think straight. Everything I thought I wanted went to shit, Dani."

"No. It didn't. *Marc* went to shit. The rest of your life is intact. Take a few days to shake this off and keep going. Fuck Marc. You can still do this, Nati."

I rub my eyes and let her words slide over me. I'm in complete shut-down mode. Nothing penetrates. I guess I will have to think about what this all means later. Right now, I just want to go back to sleep. I tell her that, and she eyes me for a long moment, then nods.

"Zack and I are going out tonight. Derek has a friend in town, and they're throwing a party."

"I think I'll just stay here, Dani. I'm really tired."

She leaves me be and heads to the shower. When she comes back from her shift a few hours later, it's past eleven. I can't believe how much I slept, and how tired I still am. Dani insists I go to the party, but I tell her I just want to go back to sleep.

And I do.

I wake up early on Sunday morning. It's a little past seven and the sun is beginning to stretch behind the mountains. On the desk, my phone shows ten missed calls from Marc, and a new list of text messages, also from him. I turn the power off and toss it on my bed, then peek through the blinds of our small window. The sky is a canvas of pink and indigo. It's really breathtaking. Dani is still asleep and I don't wake her, knowing she probably came back only a couple of hours ago. I quietly get into my ski clothes. I pick up my ski boots and hesitate for a moment, contemplating taking them to the dumpster instead. I don't want anything that reminds me of Marc. But then I decide I won't let him fuck with my life any more than he already has. The ski boots stay.

Derek is at the lower chair getting ready to open when I show up with my skis on my shoulder. He's surprised to see me, but smiles.

"Early bird gets the worm. You missed one hell of a poker game last night."

I give him a small smile. "I figured you needed to grow your savings, Derek."

His answering grin lights up his whole face. "I did. Liam was sick, and Zack pulled out after the first round. I made a hundred bucks."

"That's great," I mumble. "Are you opening this soon?" I say, clipping my boots into my skis.

"Yup. All ready for ya'." He presses a few buttons inside the small cabin, and the chair lift comes to life. I wait at the mark, then slide into the seat that approaches.

"Later," I say, lowering my goggles. He smiles at me and waves, watching me as I get lifted off the base.

The mountain is deserted. As the chair makes its leisure journey to the summit I lean my helmet against the side bar, watching the waking sun gleam on the snow. The valley looks almost like a child's picture of winter, pine trees covered in new snow underneath white mountain peaks. Once I reach the top I slide off the chair and take a lungful of chilled air. I'm the only skier so far, and I can't help thinking that I'm as alone and cold out here as I feel inside.

With Marc out of the picture, I don't know what my future will be. Dread swims in my stomach. I know he's feeling like shit, and that I should probably do the mature thing by answering his calls, so we can talk this through. But I already know there is nothing he can say to change what happened. To me, cheating in a relationship is out of the question completely. Even if I eventually forgave him, I don't think I could ever trust him again. And an adult conversation is not going to change the fact that he's a cheating prick. So to hell with that.

The other chair lifts are still not open, so my only option at the moment is to ski down the back of the mountain to the base. It will take a little over an hour, and there are several areas where I can find powder. I'm craving the physical exertion to ease the weight in my chest.

As I go down the second black diamond, I'm faced with the Women's Downhill run. I stop at the top, and watch the snow disappear behind a steep narrow path downhill and into the first sharp turn. I stare at it for a long moment, my panting breaths coming out in broken vapor. My hands grip the poles and I clench my teeth, then squeeze my eyes shut as the panic churns in my stomach, sending a cold chill down my back. *Dammit*.

Once again, it beats me. And I can't.

I push myself off to the side and cut across the trail, leaving the Women's Downhill and the sour memories from that night, behind.

By the time I make it back to the base, my legs are shaking. I welcome the sensation, and drop onto a bench by the employee entrance to catch my breath. I remove my helmet and gloves and unbuckle my ski boots. My hair is stuck to my face with sweat and my face is wet from the melting snow I picked up on the way down. I lean back on the wall and let the burn in my muscles expand. Shane steps out of the lodge and lights up a cigarette. *Fuckdammit*. These guys and their smokes. He turns and takes in my appearance, frowning.

"Did you just come back from the top?"

I answer with a nod.

"Shit. Take it easy. You look like you dove straight into the powder."

I shrug. "It was fun."

"How fast were you going? The base hasn't been open that long."

"I don't know. See you later." I push myself off the bench and the muscles in my legs scream when I reach down for my helmet and gloves. Shane watches me leave, shaking his head.

I ask Lane if I can take my shift back. I'll go crazy without work to keep me busy. I tell her I'll still work Monday and Tuesday like we agreed, and will switch my days off with another girl. She seems happy with the new arrangement. I consider going to the pool, but the idea of being in that death trap by myself depresses me, so I go over to the tubing area and help Melanie and Jessica, who I know will welcome a change in their routine. They take turns getting hot chocolate while I look after their station, selling overpriced tickets to a group of rich teens.

That night my shift is a blur. I just zombie through it. Dani rescues me a couple of times, when she realizes I've mixed up two of the orders. Zack is already up to speed with the Marc situation, compliments of Dani. Most of the time, Zack is like well water. His emotions are secured behind the iron front he puts up. But I know better. Behind that front is a mercurial temper and anyone that pisses Zack off doesn't do it a second time. Marc is the newest member on his shit list. Zack shakes his head as he fills my drink order.

"What I wouldn't give to get my hands on that fucker," he mutters.

"That's sweet of you, Zack. But let's just...not talk about him, okay? Keep me distracted." I force a smile, and after a long pause, he gives me a nod.

A group dressed in ski clothes slides into a table in my section. They're peeling off their jackets and gear, shaking off the helmet hairdos. I pick up my tray and head in their direction to take their order. One of the girls has her arm around a guy's neck and she leans over for a kiss. I have to look away, because right now, watching a couple happily in love makes me want to hit someone. For all I know, the guy she's kissing is a cheater, like Marc. *Jesus.* I'm starting to sound like those women who think all men are bastards. Even though, at the moment, I think most of them are.

As they order their drinks, one of the guys appraises me so bluntly you'd think I'm naked. I want to swat him with my tray, but I refrain because I need my job more than ever, so I ignore him.

I return with the drinks, and the same guy tries to get my attention, asking me if I know what the best night time runs are. I tell him I have no idea, even though I know the mountain like the back of my hand. Screw him. He's probably a cheater, too. Crap, I *am* angry. Maybe a day off from work wouldn't be a bad idea if I don't want to get fired.

They order appetizers, and I let them know I'll be back shortly. Luckily, my other tables are just a group of women and two older couples.

A few minutes later, I load the food onto my tray and head over toward the first group. As I approach, I see the guy that was kissing the girl before, standing next to her. Whatever he's saying to her is holding her full attention, as well as the attention of the whole table. I'm vaguely curious, and keep my eyes on him. Then he suddenly drops to one knee. I freeze.

No he's not.

His back is to me, and even though I don't see his face, I know he's smiling as he retrieves something from his pocket. Then the four words I hate the most in this world come out of his mouth.

Will.

You.

Marry.

Me.

I can't breathe. My throat is swollen shut, and I'm pretty sure now that this is a nightmare. One of those where you show up to school naked and everyone laughs. I know it's that dream because the whole lounge is now staring at me. My eyes, wide with shock, sweep the room, then flicker to my feet, which are covered with a slimy substance that looks a lot like the buffalo chicken sauce from the appetizer I was carrying a minute ago. Dani appears at my side, and takes quick inventory of the situation. Her expression falls when she sees the guy still on one knee.

"Jesus. Let's go," she says.

I say nothing, and let her pull me away as one of the other waitresses approaches with a broom.

"I shouldn't have let you come to work today, Nati. I'm sorry. Sometimes I totally suck as a friend."

I shake my head. Words fail me, and I begin to cry as she tugs me into the back supply area.

"Are you alright?" She grimaces, because I'm obviously not.

"I'm so sorry, Dani." I wipe my tears furiously. I hate that I'm crying. Then I try to push past her, but she stops me. I look up at her worried eyes. "I have to go clean that up."

"Don't worry about that." She frowns. "Tate's got it." She then lets out a heavy sigh. "Natalia. Take the rest of the shift off. I'll tell Sarah you're sick. Tate and I will cover for you."

I shake my head. "No. I can handle it."

She gives me a pitiful look that tells me she knows I can't. "Go work out. Don't go skiing, but maybe a workout will be good. Or just open one of the bottles we brought from the party last night and get shitfaced. I'll join you as soon as I'm done."

I give her a slight nod. She's right. I can't handle the rest of my shift. Not if I want to keep my job.

I lumber back to my room. I can't go work out if I'm supposed to be sick enough to leave mid-shift. I also don't feel like getting drunk by myself, which doesn't leave me with a lot of options.

On my bed, my cell phone lights up, showing another string of text and voice messages from Marc. I send it flying across the room and watch it crash against the wall. I immediately realize how stupid that was. That solves the Marc message problem, but I won't get any calls from the internship hotel either. I clutch my hair and drop on the bed face down, then let myself cry hard. I cry for what feels like a long time, and at some point, I fall asleep.

As I stir, a tug around my waist wakes me. I reach down, and realize my apron is tangled underneath me. I'm still wearing my work uniform. The room is dark, just faint slanted threads of moonlight filtering through the closed blinds. Dani is still not back. I go to the bathroom and get into my PJs before going back to bed.

I lie under the covers, staring at the ceiling. I'm sick of being in this room, and am now wide awake from the long nap. The clock says its eleven in the evening. Chances are most of the evening staff is still working and Sarah, the manager, has left for the day. Without a second thought, I dash to the closet and pull out my ski clothes.

Half an hour later, I'm flying down the familiar night runs, feeling free for the first time since I left. It's freezing, and the wind is picking up, so I need to hurry if I want to make it down to the base before the visibility is fully gone.

The familiar fatigue pulses in my legs, enhanced by my early visit to the slopes this morning, so I decide to take a safe way down. But as I traverse across, I'm faced once again with the Women's Downhill. There is a full moon and the snow is bathed in a fluorescent glow. I repeat what I did this morning and stand, staring at the run that disappears into a sharp turn. And sure enough, the fear rises from within.

I pull out the flask I stuck in my pocket, and take a long swig of vodka. It burns as it slides down my throat, and I do it again. I'm not suicidal, but for some reason today seems like the right day to face the rest of my fears full on, and a sip or two of vodka will boost my courage.

My first fear was that I might someday lose Marc. I realize now, that it wasn't only him I feared losing, but the promise of the life I had always dreamed of. A life with all the safety that comes with money, and the security of eternal love. For a moment, I wonder which I will miss the most. I laugh out loud because finally admitting this makes me the most pathetic person I've ever known. I take another swig of vodka, and wipe my mouth with the back of my glove. Cold sweat trickles down my back as I stare down at the run.

Fuck it.

I push myself off the edge and bolt down the run at blazing speed. It is icy, so I'm going even faster than it's probably safe, but the courage from the alcohol erases all thoughts of potential risks.

I fly down, and it almost feels good, like I'm giving life the finger. The run is decently well lit by the moonlight, and it vaguely diminishes the fear gripping my gut. Every muscle in my body is tense, focused only on what lies ahead. Needles of arctic air pierce my cheeks and lips, but the fear sends me flying forward.

I make the first turn, and nearly lose my balance. I don't dwell on it, and I don't slow down. The run is icy in the areas where the sun has melted the snow in the morning and I try to steer to the opposite sides. But it's dark, and the blazing speed I'm building makes it harder and harder to stay on top of every move I make. As I take the third turn, the excessive ice buildup causes me to lose my balance again. I half recover, but the momentum throws me off.

The next five seconds happen in slow motion.

Tango's face flashes in my head as my weight shifts backward for a split second. It is just enough to cause the edge of my ski to brush against a tree branch. I veer to dodge the tree, and whip sideways, my helmet bouncing hard against the ice. I'm sliding face down at full speed, desperate to grip anything that will stop me. There's nothing and as I go down my gloves scrape the surface of the ice, sending shards of white crystals against my face. I slide down for what feels like an eternity. I've lost both my skis somewhere behind and not even my poles tangled around my wrists can slow me down. I hit a bump and something hard slams against my back. A sharp tug on my wrists yanks me to a stop.

Pain lances through me.

I can't move.

Both my hands are handcuffed by my pole straps onto a protruding tree branch. I manage to raise my head, and shake the snow off my face so I can breathe. Luckily, it clears off easily. I vainly tug on my restraints. They burn as they cut the skin on my wrists. My whole body burns with exhaustion as I fight to turn around so I'm facing up. Fire stretches down my arms and I slump my head back, letting the last few seconds register. My head is throbbing, and my body is limp. Raw fear expands in my chest as I rack my brain for a way out. The only thing I know for sure is that I'm royally fucked. It's so cold. The numbness seeps into me like ink.

I close my eyes and let the darkness win.

Chapter 14: *Jake*

With all the paperwork signed and the plans approved I have nothing left to do in San Diego. Pete and I spend Saturday surfing at Swami's, then visit the local surf shops to assess the competition. In the evening, we go out to Union Bar for drinks. It's swarming with locals, and the atmosphere is fun and carefree. I know I'm going to like living in San Diego. It still keeps some of that authentic spirit of the old California that is already erased in L.A. Sydney stayed at home with the baby, so it's just the two of us. Several women approach us and try starting a conversation, but it's guys night and Pete is married, so he smiles at them as he lifts his left hand to show off his ring. I'm relieved. The only thing in my mind is how much I want to see Natalia. I imagine her playing poker with the staff and it makes me smile. She's probably wiping them out. I listen to the woman sitting in front of me, taking sips of her cosmopolitan as she tells me about a surf spot up north. Normally, I'd be into her. She has that surfer-girl look, shabby long blond hair, golden tanned skin, even though it's winter, and large blue eyes. But an image of Natalia in that plain black one piece is messing with my head, and I have to look away. Pete shakes his head. He knows I'm fucked.

I say goodbye to Pete and Sydney Sunday morning, and head to the airport to catch a plane back to Aspen. I'm not supposed to arrive until Wednesday evening, but the urge to see Natalia has turned into a need. Fortunately, the villa I've reserved is also available tonight and tomorrow, so I book it without pondering over how much this wild goose chase for Natalia is costing me.

I scan the lobby area as I check in, knowing she's probably working her shift at the lounge. Anticipation swells in my chest and I head toward that area to surprise her. Will she be happy to see me? I smile. Despite her hesitation the last time I saw her, something tells me she will be. I enter the lounge, wondering vaguely if she has been practicing swimming while I was gone. I slide my bag off my shoulder, and take a seat at the bar. Zack acknowledges me with a nod and I order a beer. He fills a pint and slides it over. I thank him, and make eye contact before he turns back to his other orders.

"Is Natalia working tonight?"

He stills for a moment, and his eyes narrow a fraction. He seems protective of her. I wonder if they're good friends, or if he has other hopes as well.

"She has the night off," he finally says. "Why?"

I nod, feigning indifference in case he, too, is hoping for more with her. "She told me she'd be working tonight."

He eyes me for another moment. "She wasn't feeling well," he mutters. This gets my immediate attention. I lock eyes with him.

"She okay?"

"Yeah, I think so." He nods, then turns around to attend an order from Natalia's friend, Dani. I want to reach across the bar and grip him by the shirt to demand he tells me exactly what happened to Natalia. But when I look over at Dani, she's eyeing me with an amused expression. I greet her with a nod, and she acknowledges me with a smile. Zack says something to her, then rounds the bar and leaves to the back. I take the opportunity to see if Dani will give me more information.

"Hey, is Natalia okay?" I ask.

She raises her eyebrows in surprise.

"Zack told me," I say, pretending he shared more than this, and in hopes that it will make Dani trust me.

She gives me a nod, but seems skeptical. "Yeah. She went to bed early."

"Look, do you think I can see her for a minute? I've got something to tell her. Good news." I smile, hoping she won't call my act and figure out I'm full of shit. I just want to see her. Surprisingly, I seem to have said the right thing, because she gives me a half-smile and glances at her watch.

"Give me a sec." She loads her tray and delivers the drinks, then walks over to the other waitress and says something while gesturing to the table she was serving. She wipes her hands on her apron, and heads back in my direction.

"Zack, Amy is watching my table. Be back in a minute."

As he makes his way back behind the bar, Zack shoots a suspicious look at me. I smile in response, and follow Dani to the employee wing.

She tells me to wait outside their room, and unlocks the door, closing it behind her. Less than fifteen seconds later, the door swings open.

"She's not here," she sighs, running a hand through her hair.

"Where else can she be?"

She looks away and shakes her head. "Skiing. Her clothes are not here either."

"Oh." I frown, glancing at my watch. It's past eleven and the night runs will be closed soon.

"Shit." She bites her index nail, and her eyes scan the space around her.

"What's the matter? She goes skiing at night all the time."

She gives me a wary look, probably wondering how I know this, but right now I need her to trust me. I give her the most sincere, trustworthy look I can muster.

"Dani. Tell me what's wrong."

She lets out a long sigh. "She had a shitty night–weekend," she corrects herself. "She had a...fight with her fiancé and was upset."

"And?"

"She dropped a tray full of drinks, so I told her to take the rest of the night off. I told her not to go skiing, though. She was out of it."

"Are you worried?"

She looks up at me and her eyes are etched in regret. "Yes."

I dart a quick look at my watch. "The run will close in twenty minutes. Let me change and I'll go look for her."

She closes her eyes. "I can't explain right now and not that she'd be stupid enough, but check the Women's Downhill, will you?"

I frown. That run would be extremely challenging at night. "Okay."

"Thanks," she mutters. She pulls out her cell phone and we exchange our contact information. I turn to leave, but she grips my arm. "Jake...Natalia needs this job more than ever, please keep this quiet, okay?"

I nod, then dash to my room. I want to know what she meant by 'more than ever.' I also can't deny the sudden thrill I feel because she had a fight with her fiancé, and that means hope, but the need to know she's safe overpowers everything else.

I change in record time. My villa is a short distance away from the lift, and I rush over to catch my ride. Derek greets me and tells me he'll close after me. I ask him about Natalia, and he says she went up a long while ago. Unease stirs in my chest as I make the slow journey up. The night is clear, but the temperature is barely above zero. I say a silent prayer that she's okay and that she'll tease me later for worrying about her.

At the top, I comb down the areas where I've seen Natalia skiing before. I'm alert to any movement or sound, but there's nothing, just the wind whistling through the trees. I traverse across to the Women's Downhill and begin my way down, trying to slow down my speed as much as I can, but the run is icy and I'm already praying she did not come down this way. As I make the third turn, something a few feet ahead catches my attention. I slow until I come to a full stop next to it.

My chest tightens when I recognize Natalia's ski.

I quickly pick it up and slide down, looking for the other one while I call out her name. My heart is hammering. I find the other ski a few yards down, and call out for her again. The sound of my skis scraping the solid ice make it almost impossible to hear anything else. I stop to listen, then yell her name again.

A faint voice answers from somewhere down the hill and I rush toward it, stopping every few yards to call to her and listen.

"I'm here," her faint voice says from an area off the trail. I pull out a flashlight from my backpack, and secure both her skis under my left arm as I sweep the snow with the light. She's down some distance ahead, and it looks like she's tied to something, hanging from the wrists. I bolt down and drop her skis, unclipping mine so I can help her.

"Jesus, fuck. Are you okay?"

"Jake," she whimpers. Her voice is faint, and I wonder how long she's been here. Her wrists are locked by the straps on her ski poles, which are tangled around a protruding tree branch. I get closer and pull a Swiss Army knife out of my pocket.

"Babe, I'll get you out of here. Can you move?" I say as I cut through the straps at her wrists. They snap, and her arms drop limp on the snow. I'm afraid to move her, in case there is damage to her back. I should call the ski patrol, but Dani's comment about Natalia needing her job more than ever stops me.

"Baby, can you move?"

She doesn't answer, but pulls her arms down, then stirs and is able to get almost to a sitting position. This means there's no damage to her back, and I let out a sigh of relief. I pick her up and pull her onto my lap, rubbing her arms. She's shivering and when I press my face to hers I flinch. Her checks are as cold as the snow around us. I need to get her out of here before she's fully overcome by hypothermia.

"Natalia, I should call the ski patrol. They'll bring a stretcher and get you out of here."

"No." Her eyes widen slightly, then she closes them again. "Please...Jake. You help me. If anyone...knows I've been out here...I will get fired. Please. Please help me," she whispers and it seems to take the last of her strength. Her head drops to my shoulder.

I envelope her in my arms, knowing that as stupid as it is not to call the ski patrol, I will do anything she asks me. I try to share some of my body heat. She's shaking. Desperation claws its way up my chest.

"We need to get out of here. Can you walk?"

She trembles as I pull her up with me. Her clothes and boots are covered in snow, and I brush it off so she can move a little easier. I can't help her and carry both of our skis, so I stab them in the snow by a tree and wrap my arm around her waist to support her. We're not too far from the base, and I know the mountain well enough to recognize a trail that cuts down to the villa where I'm staying.

Natalia leans on me, making a huge effort to walk, but she doesn't give up. I try to come up with reassuring words to keep her focused as we make our way down. She's weak, and I know it won't be long before her body can't take anymore.

Just as we are a few yards away from my cabin, she whispers my name. As I tip my head down, she collapses and passes out.

I pick her up in my arms and carry her the rest of the way to my cabin.

And I think we are safe.

Chapter 15: *Natalia*:

I can't stop the shaking. My body convulses from hypothermia as Jake opens the door to his villa. I'm not sure if this is a dream, or if he's really here. He slides me onto the couch and immediately starts taking my clothes off. I want to help him, but my limbs are unresponsive and numb from fatigue and lying on the snow. Jake holds my face in his hands and says my name. I manage to open my eyes and he sighs, from relief, I think. His eyes are etched in worry as he says soothing words and tells me to try to stay awake.

"I'm going to fill up the bathtub, okay? I'll be back in just a second."

I don't want him to go, but I nod, leaning back onto the couch. My eyelids are heavy. I'm so tired. I let them drop, even though he told me not to.

He's back and says my name again, then holds my hands and squeezes them.

"You're so cold," he says. I feel cold, but want to tell him the cold comes from within. My jacket is off. He removes my sweatshirt and ski pants with some effort. I wish I could help, but my body feels as if it's made out of lead. He strips off the rest of my clothes until I'm left in a camisole and my underwear. I'm not wearing a bra and feel exposed, but I don't care. Jake carries me to the bathtub and slowly slips me in. The water is too hot and I gasp from the shock. Jake holds my arms and tells me it's okay. It's just warm, he says I need to get used to it. I think he's scared because he keeps repeating 'it's going to be okay. You're safe.' I lean back onto the bathtub, and he holds my hand.

"Natalia, try to stay awake, okay?"

The way he says my name brings tears to my eyes.

"Jake…"

"Shh," he says. "You're going to be fine." He pulls out his phone and calls Dani. Why is Jake calling Dani? He tells her I'm okay, then says his villa number. He tells her I need dry clothes. I'm exhausted and close my eyes while they talk. Jake doesn't let go of my hand.

A knock on the door wakes me. I startle, and Jake squeezes my hand.

"It's okay," he says. "It's just Dani. I'm going to open the door." He lets go of my hand.

I frown.

Dani barges in, and her face falls when she sees me.

"Nati. What the fuck."

"Dani," Jake interrupts. "I need to get her out of the bathtub. Then you can strip the rest of her clothes off and we can wrap her into this." He shows her a robe. Dani helps him, and they lift me out of the bathtub. I feel a little stronger and manage to stand up. Then Jake leaves and Dani seats me on the toilet. Water pours down onto the floor, and I start shaking again. Dani helps me strip naked and into the robe.

Jake comes back into the bathroom, and carries me to the couch, then wraps a blanket around me. I close my eyes. I'm just so tired.

"I'll make her some tea," he says.

"Jake. Shit. She can't walk back to the lodge like this. People will ask questions and after what happened at work today, she doesn't need that kind of attention."

"Let her stay here. She can have one of the bedrooms. I'll have her give you a call in the morning." He leaves, to make tea I think, and Dani sits next to me on the couch, assessing my condition. I'm still trembling and it seems like the warmth of all the blankets in the world wouldn't be enough. Dani brushes my hair off my forehead. "Nati. I can't get you back to our room right now. Do you want me to stay here with you? I just need to get a few things and I'll be back."

I shake my head. "It's okay. I trust Jake. You...should go. One of us...should be there. Just in case...people ask." My teeth rattle.

It takes Dani a long time, but she finally agrees to leave me at Jake's villa. She says she will be back in the morning, and tells me to call her if I need anything. I look up at her because I don't have a phone. She rolls her eyes. Obviously she knows this, since she's been in our room and most likely found the remains of my cell phone.

"Just use Jake's phone if you need me," she mutters, then kisses my forehead. "Are you sure you'll be okay? Jesus, Nati. You gave me one shit of a scare."

I nod and she sighs, then stands up and says goodbye, thanking Jake on her way out.

Jake makes quick work of lighting the fireplace by the couch where I am. He makes me drink the tea. When I'm finished, he sits beside me and wraps his arm around my back. He pulls me to him as he rubs my arm to keep me warm.

"How are you doing, Natalia?"

"Fine," I mutter and close my eyes. I just want to sleep, but the images of what happened in the last two days are overwhelming as they flash through my mind. Warm moisture fills my eyes and I start crying against Jake's chest. His arms tighten around me.

"Shh...it's okay. You're safe."

I cry harder, because I'm safe and at the same time I am not. For the first time in my life I have no idea of what I'm going to do next. All my years of careful planning, crafting a perfect future for myself, are gone. My future with Marc is gone, and I can't shake that off. I'm tired and a big part of me wants to let all the rest go to hell. Jake kisses my hair and says nothing.

We stay like that until I'm too tired to cry anymore. He begins to lift me up and says he will take me to the bedroom, but I clutch his arm.

"I want to stay here. Is that okay?"

He says it is. Then asks me if I need anything and kisses my temple.

"Can you...stay?" I ask him. Our eyes lock, and I think he feels sorry for me. I hate that he pities me, but I don't want to be alone, and right now that is all I care about. I don't want to close my eyes and see Marc, or Tango's face as I slid down that icy run, or the thoughts I had when I was lying on the snow and I thought...I just don't want to think about any of it. Jake nods and relief floods me, so I smile. His answering smile is dazzling, and for a few moments everything else moves to the background and there is only Jake. He pulls me to his chest again and lays back on the couch. It is deep enough that we can snuggle and I nestle myself against him, his arms circling around me. The heat that radiates from his body envelopes me and it feels so good I almost start crying again. I press my face to his chest and his scent invades me. He smells like suede and body wash and salty sweat. It's a heady combination and I want to bury myself into him. He kisses the top of my head.

"Jake."

"Hmm?"

"Thank you."

He kisses my head on the same spot, and I curl up against him. His hand strokes my arm rhythmically, and it's soothing. The clock on the mantel says it's one thirty in the morning, and I yawn as exhaustion claims me.

Slanted sunlight filters through the shutters of the living area of Jake's villa. I flutter my eyes open and stir slightly. My body is stiff, but Jake is still asleep at my side and I don't want to wake him. He probably had a shitty night's sleep on this couch, and he had two empty bedrooms. I look up at him and as I move his eyes open and meet mine. They are liquid amber. He smiles.

"Good morning."

"Good morning." I smile back.

"Sleep well?"

I nod. "You?"

"Yes. How do you feel?"

"Better than I deserve."

He sighs. "You scared me, Natalia."

I press my face to his chest so I don't have to look in his eyes. "I'm sorry."

He strokes my hair and I close my eyes.

"You want to tell me about it?"

Normally, I'd say no. I don't talk about my feelings to anyone, except Dani. It makes me uncomfortable, and I don't think it's anyone's business. But I do want to tell Jake. It surprises me, and I don't fully get why I want to tell him about it, but I do.

"That night, when you and I said goodbye after our date, I felt like I needed to see Marc. It had been a while, and I guess I needed the reassurance that what we had was real. So I bought a ticket to L.A. I wanted to surprise him." I let out a humorless chuckle. "I surprised him, alright. A half-naked chick wearing only his T-shirt opened the door."

"Seriously?" He frowns and his jaw locks.

"Seriously." I sigh.

"Then what?"

"Then...I told him he was a cheating son of a bitch and walked away."

"And he just let you go?"

"There was a cop on the street, and he told Marc to leave me be. I went back to the airport, but the first flights were not till the morning."

"You spent the night at the airport?"

I shrugged. "Honestly, it didn't really matter at that point."

His arms squeeze me. He kisses the top of my head.

"I'm sorry, Natalia."

"It's ironic, Jake. How I thought there was something wrong with you, because you have no expectations when it comes to relationships. It is actually genius."

He lets out a long sigh. "No, Natalia. It is not. It's lonely."

I look up at him and his expression tells me that last thing slipped out.

"I would give anything, *anything*, not to feel the way I'm feeling right now, ever again. It's not worth it, Jake. And you know what's worse? It isn't the fact that I won't be with Marc for the rest of my life that hurts the most. I realize now that it's letting go of the dream of the life we would have had together. That's fucked up, isn't it?"

"Do you love him?"

I frown. "Yes. I do. I...*did*, actually. I don't think I could ever look at him the same way I did before. Something broke inside of me that night. It can't be put back together."

Jake nods. "Deception is a tricky thing. I actually know exactly how you feel. That's why I chose to live my life the way I do."

"And you're smart. Love is highly overrated." I pull myself up and he's watching me with a pensive expression. I want to ask him what happened to him that makes him understand how I feel. But I don't. He said he's a very private person and I don't want to pry.

"Coffee?" I ask to lighten the mood.

Jake makes coffee, and I call Dani to let her know I'm okay and that I'll wait for the morning shift to begin, to avoid running into the other employees on their way to work. Jake and I sit at the kitchen nook to have our coffee. Outside, the snow is shimmering under the morning sun. The view from these villas is spectacular. The resort charges a small fortune for them and now I know why.

We have an easy conversation, and he's not happy when I tell him I didn't practice swimming. I have decided to go forward with my internship, so we make plans to meet after my shift that afternoon for a swimming session. I'm working noon to four, so it gives him plenty of time to do other things. He says he will hike back to the spot where he left our skis, and will bring them back to his villa. I pack my ski clothes in a garbage bag he gives me, and look up at him.

"You were supposed to come back Wednesday. What changed?"

He shrugs. "I had a couple of people to meet in downtown Aspen." He doesn't make eye contact and doesn't explain further. I wonder if 'people' means *clients*. I squash the thought because the idea of Jake with other women is revolting to me. I don't know why it bothers me so much, but it does. I don't want to think about Jake's line of work right now.

"See you later?" I smile as he holds the door open for me. His answering smile sends a whirlpool to my stomach. I lean over and give him a kiss on the cheek.

"Later," he says, and he's still smiling.

I work my shift, feeling almost normal for the first time since I came back. The Marc nightmare is starting to fade to the background, and even though I'm two-thirds full of dread, it seems to be receding. I also don't want to admit that the other third of me is filled with thoughts of Jake. Jake is a dead end, and even though he rescued me from death, he's far from being a knight on a white horse. But I'd be lying if I said that knowing I will meet with him after my shift is not making me smile more than I should be smiling after breaking up with my fiancé.

I'm waiting at the pool at four thirty sharp, like we agreed. Jake shows up wrapped in a robe like the one he put on me last night. *Maybe it's the same one?* I'm bundled in a long parka, sitting on the edge of the pool with my feet in the water. It's like 90 degrees in the pool and it feels heavenly. I give him a little wave and he smiles. He looks like a Greek Adonis, all six feet four of him in that long white robe. He sits next to me and kisses my cheek. My heart wakes up.

"Ready?" he says. I nod and shrug off my parka. He does the same, and gets into the water first, then holds my hand to pull me in. I still.

"Come on, chicken. You have this part down, remember?"

I smirk, but oblige.

Jake is all business today. He makes me stretch my arms in front of me and grip the edge of the pool while I kick with my feet. He stays close and makes corrections. I feel safe because he's standing right next to me, and I'm no longer afraid I will drown.

Somehow, being so close to my death last night has significantly diminished my fear of drowning. I know I owe that to Jake, so I want to make his time worthwhile, and show him I can do this.

He gives me a foam board, and tells me to practice kicking while he swims right by my side. He seems so at ease in the water, and I envy him. I can tell he loves it. He smiles and he looks so handsome, I get distracted more than once.

Next, I stand and watch while he shows me the freestyle movement of the arms. He makes me practice it at the shallow end, and once I've got it down he tells me it's time to put it all together. I'm nervous, but Jake reassures me that I've got this. I begin by pushing myself off the wall, and practice what he's taught me. At first, I'm overcome by a sudden panic that I will sink, but Jake places his palm under my stomach and supports me. Before I know it, he's pulled it away and I'm freaking doing it. I push the water backward with my cupped hands like he showed me and don't stop until I meet the wall at the deep end. I hold on to the edge of the pool, panting and grinning.

"I did it, Jake! I can swim. OMG!"

Jake's smile is disarming, and I have to fight the urge to kiss him because I'm so freaking happy, and it feels good to be sharing this moment with him.

I swim to the other side and he makes me practice it several times. When we finish, I'm panting, and only halfway full of Marc-dread and half full of happiness and Jake.

"Thank you," I say, looking up at him.

"You're welcome. I'm proud of you, Natalia. You've got this."

The way he says my name combined with the fact that I just made him proud makes my chest swell. I jump and wrap my arms around his neck, startling him. His arms close around me, and we hug each other for a few silent seconds. I suddenly realize how much more intimate this is, because we are only wearing bathing suits. I slowly pull away and meet his eyes. I see pride in their caramel background. He's got amazing eyes.

"Let's celebrate," he says. "Tonight. Dinner at my place."

I open my mouth to question whether that's a good idea, but he stops me.

"We already spent the night together, and there's no risk of feelings being misunderstood, so dinner and a movie would be fun if you're up to it. My friends get here tomorrow, and I won't have the place to myself anymore."

I smile, but can't help a pang of disappointment. I don't want our feelings misunderstood, but I also can't help how much I like spending time with Jake. Dinner and a movie seem safe and exactly what I need at the moment, so I agree. He hands me my parka and out of the corner of my eye I see someone approaching. I look up, and my whole body freezes at once.

Marc.

He is completely dressed in black. Armani, no doubt. His face is serious and determined as he gets closer. I frown. He's the last person I want to see right now, and I also don't want Marc to be a part of my memories in Aspen. At all. As far as I'm concerned Marc is a memory-wrencher.

He stops a few steps away, and his clear blue eyes lock on Jake, trying to assess the situation.

"What are you doing here?" I snarl.

"I need to talk to you and you don't answer my calls." His tone is calm, and that makes me madder. I look up at Jake and his eyes are burning a hole on Marc. Jake turns to me and his whole face is drawn in fury. His hand flexes into a fist.

"You okay?" he says, ignoring Marc, who is now looking at him full-on.

I glance up at Marc and nod, even though I want him to leave. In my mind, we are over, and nothing he says will change that. But maybe this is inevitable, and we need to have closure.

Jake gives Marc another murderous glare and tells me he'll see me later. He swiftly pulls himself out of the water, then walks away.

"I'm cold," I say to Marc. "Let me change." I tell him to get his car and that I will meet him at the curb. I don't want to talk to Marc here, because this is my workplace and I maxed out on drama last night. He frowns, but agrees.

We drive a few miles, and stop by a small rest area with a viewpoint of the valley. It's breathtaking and in other circumstances it would be extremely romantic. Marc kills the engine and turns to me.

"I'm so sorry, Natalia. Can we just...start over?"

I frown. "Just like that? Start over?"

"I'm in love with you." He reaches for my hand and I pull it away.

"You have a funny way to show love, Marc." I look up at him with narrow eyes. "How could you? How could you fucking cheat on me? I would *never* do that to you. You ruined everything."

"You're right. I'm sorry. The truth is that this whole long-distance thing has been much harder than I thought."

"That's your excuse? It was *hard*? You could've told me before. We could've worked something out."

"Really? Like what?" he snaps. "You're so wrapped up into working and getting the internship. Every minute in your life is accounted for, Natalia. I got the feeling we would never reach a point where it was just you and me. I need you by my side. I want you to be my *wife*. The rest has to come second to that."

"Are you kidding? You were *fucking* someone else TWO FUCKING DAYS AGO."

"She doesn't mean anything."

"Stop saying that. It just makes it worse. All it means is that you couldn't keep your dick in your pants. Tell me something. How many were there?"

"What?"

"How many women, Marc? I want to know."

He looks disconcerted, and his eyes dart to the picturesque view outside. And I have my answer. But I want to hear it from his lying, cheating lips.

"Tell me."

"I don't know. What does it matter? I want to marry *you*. That won't happen again, Natalia."

"You're damn right it won't. Because I don't ever want to see you again." A knot swells in my throat, and burning tears are streaming down my cheeks. He tries to pull me into a hug and I start hitting him with my fists and calling him a liar and a cheater. He is way stronger than me and grips me hard against his chest, wrapping his arms around me. It's uncomfortable because we are pressed against each other in the confined space of the car. I stop fighting him and cry. Hard. Marc kisses my hair and asks me to forgive him, over and over. He pleads for another chance. I still love him, and part of me wonders if another chance can save us. Maybe I can learn to forgive. Any option seems better than the pain this is causing me. But despite the jagged meteorite churning in my chest, I know.

This is the end of us.

Chapter 16: *Jake*

I go downtown and pace around. I need to think and let the rage from the last ten minutes flow. Plus I told Natalia I had people to see, which was complete bullshit, but now I need to keep appearances. I wander aimlessly around the small town. The sky is overcast, and the streets are painted with fresh snow. People walk in and out of restaurants, bundled up and looking happy to be out in the high season of Aspen.

At a liquor store, I buy a couple of bottles of wine for my dinner with Natalia tonight. I wonder if we still have a date. With the turn things took, who the fuck knows. I may be drinking alone.

It starts to snow, so I grab a coffee, then go into a couple of art galleries to kill time. I'm soon out of distractions, and can't take my mind off this afternoon. I want to know what happened between Natalia and that shithead. Not that I blame him for showing up, I would've done the same. But I sure as hell hope he's still downgraded to ex-fiancé. Why in the fuck any guy would cheat on a woman like Natalia, is beyond me.

I take a cab back to the lodge and shower. It's almost eight in the evening, and I wish I'd asked Natalia for her number, so I can check if she's still coming. I feel like a goddamn teen before my first date with the girl I've got a crush on. I pour myself a scotch and down it. *Easy, Jake. No false expectations, remember?*

Half an hour later, there's a knock on the door and I rush to it. I run both hands through my hair and take a deep breath, laughing at myself. When I open the door, she's there, dressed in a white turtleneck and jeans. She looks beautiful, and I love that she's not trying to impress me, and chose to wear something comfortable. She smiles as she kisses my cheek and walks in. I fucking love Argentina and their greeting customs.

"I brought popcorn," she says, handing me a couple of pouches of microwavable stuff.

"Great." I follow her in. She looks calm and I want to ask her about this afternoon. The fact that she's here with popcorn is a good sign that she and the cheating fuck didn't get back together, so I relax. I hand her a room service menu and tell her we can choose a movie while we wait for the food. She likes my plan, and tells me she's starving. I love that she's hungry and that she didn't eat before our date, like most women would have. I order our dinner, and reach into the fridge for the bottle of sauvignon blanc I bought this afternoon. I pour two glasses and we toast to her new swimming abilities. She laughs and thanks me for the millionth time.

"It's okay, you can ask me," she says, plopping down on the couch as she sips the last of her wine.

"What?"

"You're not curious as to how my afternoon went?"

Yes. I'm in fucking agony. I shrug. "I figured you would tell me if you wanted to talk about it." I place a few logs into the fireplace and light it. The fire crackles as it comes to life. She lets out a long sigh.

"He wants another chance. He promised it will never happen again."

I nod. "What do you think?"

She rolls her eyes. "Seriously, Jake. How stupid do you think I am? The worst part is that I asked him how many women there have been, and he had to look away."

"Asshole," I mutter.

"*Yeah*. He is an asshole. It sucks. I guess I'm glad it happened now and not in a few years when we had a family. But it hurts, you know? I wish it didn't hurt this much, but it does." Her eyes are full of pain, and I close my hands into fists. I swear if I had that motherfucker in front of me right now, I'd make him swallow his teeth. Despite the front she's trying to put up, Natalia looks heartbroken, and there's nothing I wouldn't do to take that pain away.

"I'm sorry." I sit next to her on the couch and take her hand. She stares at the fire, and a sad smile stretches on her face. "That was my first fear. That Marc would leave me. The other one was to go down the Women's Downhill."

"How come?"

"I had a childhood friend. Tango. We became soul mates the day we met. We were only seven. His dad was a mean drunk and his mom had passed, so even though we didn't have much, he practically lived at my house. My mom loved him, sometimes I think more than she loved me, but that's okay. Tango had nobody.

"He always pushed me to do things I was afraid of doing. He said I had to toughen up and be brave so I could take care of myself. Tango spent a lot of time on the streets. He was smart. So smart. He was a hell of a poker player, too." She laughs.

"Ah. So that's where those ruthless skills came from."

She nods, smiling. "Yup. He was a good teacher. Beat me at everything. Even as we got older, the only things I could do better than him were cooking and skiing. He teased me when I came to work up here for the season. He always wished he could ski, but couldn't afford it. We used to watch the winter Olympics on TV. He dared me to become a better skier, said I needed to ski the black diamonds for him. Two years ago, I had finally saved enough for his airline ticket and a season pass. I was going to surprise him. But while I was up here I found out he had dropped out of law school and hadn't told me anything. I was so angry with him."

"Wait. *Law* school? How could he afford that?"

"Public colleges are free in Argentina. Some of them are the best. Especially law school. Becoming a lawyer doesn't cost you a dime."

"Are you serious?"

She nods. "He would have made an amazing lawyer. I wanted that for him, so badly. Anyway, every year I came here and Tango stayed in Buenos Aires. We Skyped at night and he would dare me to take on the Women's Downhill. That was our thing." She smiles. "Daring each other. He knew I was terrified of it. So I said I would do it if he went back to school and finished. He gave me a hard time, but finally agreed. That morning, I made myself take on the run and Tango took the bus downtown to fill out the registration." She stops and tears pool in her eyes. "He never made it to the school building. A bus hit him full on as he was crossing the street. When I came to the base Dani told me. The hospital found my number in his cell phone and she answered." She's crying harder, and it kills me to see her like this. I put my arm around her and rub her back. "If I hadn't pushed him to do that, he would still be alive. I lost my best friend on a fucking dare."

"Natalia, babe. You can't blame yourself for that. You were pushing him to be better, just like you said he did with you. That's what you do when you love somebody." I squeeze her against me and she sobs softly on my shoulder.

"I've never been able to ski that run since. I only see him. That's why I went there last night. I wanted to lose my other fear."

I tilt her chin up, and wipe her tears with my thumbs, then pull her to me and press a kiss to her lips. They're so soft. She closes her eyes and doesn't push me away. I want to kiss her again, but I refrain, because what she needs right now is a friend.

"Come on," I tell her. "You've been through a lot the last few days. You need a break."

She nods. "Yeah. I'm sorry. I'm usually not this depressing."

There's a knock on the door and a voice announces room service. Natalia doesn't want the staff to see her here, so she leaves to the bathroom. I let the guy in and sign the bill. When she comes back, I have rolled the table with the food to the dining area. She sits and I fill her wine glass almost to the top.

"Are you trying to get me drunk?" She laughs.

"Absolutely."

She shakes her head. "I won't stop you. I think I need it."

We have dinner in comfortable silence. Afterwards, we bring the second bottle of wine to the couch, and she starts scanning through the channels while I step over to the kitchen to make the popcorn.

"Just rent whatever you want. I don't think you'll find anything on TV," I tell her.

"OMG. Silver Linings Playbook. Can we watch this?"

I frown. "Haven't you seen that already? It's been out for a while."

"Yes. And I love it. Can we watch it, please?" She turns around in the couch and smiles, bringing her hands together in a pleading gesture. It makes me smile.

"Yeah. Whatever you want. Doesn't matter to me what we watch."

She cheers and gets it set up while I pour the popcorn into a bowl.

We sit side by side with the bowl tucked between our legs. Our hands accidentally touch now and then, and it makes me want to kiss her. Everything about her makes me want to kiss her. Her body so close to mine, her warmth, the alluring scent of her perfume. It's all torture and it's a good thing I've seen the movie before because I'm not paying attention at all. I'm only aware of her and every movement or sound she makes. Our shoes are off and our feet are propped on the coffee table. She laughs at something in the movie, and turns her head to meet my eyes.

"Thanks, Jake. I'm glad I'm here." She nudges my foot with hers. I angle mine so our feet are touching.

"I'm glad you're here, too." I slide my hand down and it leans on hers. She stretches her hand out and I reflexively take it and interlace our fingers. She doesn't say anything and doesn't pull it away. She just looks at our hands together. It feels good.

And I want to kiss her.

The movie ends, and she lets out a long sigh. "Well, I better get going."

But as she gets up, I tug on our still interlaced hands.

"Don't go," I whisper. She sits back on the couch and looks up at me.

"It's kind of late."

"I don't want you to go. Stay a little longer."

"Okay. What are we going to do?"

I look into her eyes. "I want to kiss you."

Her lips part a fraction and she inhales. I know she feels something, too.

"Stay," I whisper. She looks conflicted.

"Jake. I had a shitty weekend. I need to process. Staying here and *kissing* you...would not be a very good idea."

I laugh. "You always say that."

"Say what?"

"I ask you out, or invite you to dinner and you tell me it may not be a good idea."

She blushes and shrugs, and it's adorable.

"Natalia. I want to spend more time with you, and we don't have much left." I brush her hand with the tips of my fingers. "I know you just broke up with that asshole and all that. But it doesn't have to be complicated. I just want to be with you." I bite hard at the sound of my own words. *Who's the asshole, Jake?*

She looks down at our hands for a long moment, then up at me. "Okay."

A sudden rush floods me. "Okay?"

"Yes. I want to kiss you, too. No false promises. Just now. I've never done anything for just now. My entire life has always been planned. I'm tired of it. So kiss me, Jake."

Before she has time to change her mind, I take her face in my hands and bring her mouth to mine. The moment our lips touch, I forget everything that's ever happened before this moment, and get lost in the amazing feeling of my mouth exploring hers. She's soft, and warm, and incredible. Her tongue is still cold from the wine, and I pull her closer to fully taste her. Her hands move to my shoulders, and she climbs onto my lap, straddling me. I press the small of her back toward me as my other hand holds the back of her head. My dick is at war with my jeans, and I scoot to the edge of the seat to bring her body closer. She molds to me, pressing against my hard-on and it's fucking torture because now I need to be inside her. My hands slip under her sweater, and explore every inch of her. I cup her breasts and she presses them against me. She wants this and all the visions and fantasies I've had since we first met invade me and I can't get enough. She grips my sweater and pulls it over my head. I help her, then we do the same with hers. I unclasp her bra and her skin is so incredibly soft under my hands I can't stop touching her. I trail open mouth kisses along her jaw and she arches her head back to give me better access to her neck.

"Jake," she breathes and the sound rips through me.

She stands up to strip off her jeans, but I beat her to it. Meanwhile, her fingers find the button on my jeans, and she pulls them down. Once we are both naked, I pick her up and crush her into a kiss as she wraps her legs around my waist. She's beautiful, and perfect, and I can't wait until she's mine. I take her to the bedroom and lower her to the bed, then reach to the night table for a condom while she pulls the covers off.

She watches me roll the condom on, and the way she's looking at me with her eyes half open makes me harder. She bites her lip in appreciation, then looks up.

"I'm on the pill, Jake. So if everything is alright with you, then we're good." Those emerald eyes are dark, and her hair is fanned out in a black mane over my pillow. I pause for a moment to admire her, and get rid of the condom. I'm one lucky fuck.

"I get tested regularly. We're good."

"Good," she says and her voice is husky with want. I lower myself to her, and cover her mouth with mine as I press our bodies together. My dick is so hard it hurts, but I make myself wait. I want this to be for her. I want her to feel everything, the way she deserves. My mouth sails down her neck to her breasts. I suck on them gently, taking turns. Then, I move down to her stomach, and as my tongue slides down, I can't get over how soft her skin is. She moans and arches her back, saying my name. It's so intoxicating I have to work hard to fight the urge to be inside her right this moment. I wrap my hands around her thighs and part them, then my mouth moves between her legs and she lets out a loud moan. She's so wet, and my tongue easily slides between her lips. She groans and clutches the sheet at her sides. I find her sweet spot and I'm relentless, torturing her as I slide two fingers inside her. She cries and clutches my hair, pressing me to her as she climbs, gripping me harder.

"Jake, God," she cries as her body convulses into a spiraling orgasm. I pull myself up and let her kiss her arousal, covering her mouth with mine as I lower myself into her.

And I'm lost.

Everything else fades, and it's just the two of us, now. I bury myself in her, and forget every feeling I've ever had for a woman. She's a goddess, and I can't get enough. Her body is tight and she molds to me seamlessly as I thrust in and out of her. I'm close, so I slow down and let her feel me deeper. She groans, her chest is heaving in broken breaths.

"Jake, please."

I smother her mouth and start moving faster, giving her exactly what she wants. She makes delicious sounds, and I want to absorb every one of them. I can't hold on much longer and when she starts tightening around me I tell her to let go. We come hard together and it's deep and intense and it scares the shit out of me. I never let myself lose control when I'm fucking a woman, but with her, it's so much more.

I roll off of her. We're both breathing hard.

"That. Was. Amazing." She laughs and pants. It is so beautiful and carefree that I'm afraid to open my eyes.

Because I know this kind of feeling doesn't really exist.

Chapter 17: *Natalia*:

I lie on Jake's bed, completely spent. Holy fucking Christ. Who would have thought casual sex could feel this good. I close my eyes, catching my breath. Yeah, relationships are definitely overrated. I turn my head and smile at Jake. He's catching his breath, too. He's facing the ceiling with his eyes closed. My smile widens. Casual, fun, sex-god, no-expectations-Jake. Fucking mind-blowing.

I squeeze his hand and his eyes open. He turns to me, but he's not smiling. *What's wrong?* A fleeting emotion crosses his eyes, and I think it's fear. *How odd.* But then he smiles, and it's gone.

"How do you feel?" he says.

I roll onto my side and run my fingers along the ripped lines of his torso. He's beautiful, every muscle outlined.

"That was incredible, Jake." I'm suddenly overcome by a gripping grief as to the real reason why this was so good. Blowing women's expectations off the charts is what Jake does for a living. I close my eyes, pushing away the unwelcome thought as I plop back on the bed.

"Hey." His fingers brush lose strands of hair off my face. "You okay?"

"Yes." I force myself to smile. I have no right to feel anything but appreciation for Jake and what we just did. No ties and no feelings is what I wanted, and surely what I need right now. Tango used to tell me to punch my fears on the chin. So that's exactly what I do.

"Let's do that again, Jake."

He arches an eyebrow, then smiles and rolls on top of me. His fingers stroke my face and he kisses me tenderly. The savage desperation we had for each other minutes ago is appeased, and replaced by careful appreciation. We explore every inch of each other, feel each other. No rush. We take our time with the now and let the hours melt.

Faint sunlight filters in through the shutters of Jake's room. The nightstand clock says it's almost seven in the morning. Jake sleeps peacefully next to me. We only fell asleep a few hours ago. He looks younger, and the sharp lines of his nose and profile seem softer in the dim light of the morning. His eyelashes are deep black, endless, perfectly fanned over his cheeks. I watch him sleep for a few moments, wondering if he did this for me. Last night was, without question, the best sex I've had in my entire life. Sex with Marc was good, but what I felt with Jake was fucking-mind-blowing. I wonder if I should offer him money. I don't want to insult him, but I'm not sure what the protocol is for a date with a professional escort. Saying the word, even in my thoughts leaves a sour taste, and I shake it off.

I slip out of bed, careful not to wake him, and quickly dress before making the walk of shame back to my room. I round the outside of the building, keeping my head down and fortunately don't run into any coworkers.

When I sneak into my room, Dani is already awake. She grins, taking in my appearance.

"You look thoroughly well-fucked, my friend."

"Dani!"

She laughs. "That yummy water polo god is exactly what you needed last night after you kicked that cheating douche bag to the curb. By the way, hands down you're my new hero."

I stifle a smile. "I'm glad I can serve as free entertainment for you."

"Yeah, about time you had some dirty stories of your own. I was running out. Tell me, was he good?"

I raise my palms. "I don't kiss and tell."

"Shit. *That* good? You lucky slut."

I laugh. "Dani. Your mind is rotten."

She grins proudly and nods.

I catch up on sleep while Dani goes skiing, then we get ready for our shift. I haven't had a day off in almost a week, but it doesn't matter because some of my shifts are only part-time, so the resort doesn't mind it.

Our shift starts at two, and by six o'clock the lounge is swarming with people. This will be a great night of tips and I'm glad, because I need to make up the money I spent to go see Marc. Zack, Dani and I are on a roll. Zack seems happy to see I'm back to my normal cynical self after what happened with Marc yesterday. Dani told me that when Marc showed up at the lounge, Zack kicked him out to the back, and when they came back, Marc looked ashen. Zack wouldn't tell me about it, but I gave him a tight hug anyway. I love that he always has my back.

I'm delivering drinks to a table of single guys, when I see Jake walk in with what I assume are his two friends that arrived today. They're in ski clothes, and Jake looks like one of those hot ski instructors resorts love to hire. Our eyes lock across the room and he smiles. His hair is ruffled up and he shakes it. My breath catches, and I smile back at him.

They slide into a booth in Dani's section and I ask her if I can take it. She darts a look at Jake and his friends and gives me a conspiratorial smile.

Jake's eyes are on me like lasers. He smiles as he introduces me to his friends, Pete and Dillon. They are both good-looking and already attracting attention from the women in the lounge. I smile inwardly when I see a ring on Pete's left hand. I like that Jake has a married friend.

I take their order, fighting the urge to run my hands through the beautiful mess that is Jake's chestnut hair. Wet, artfully disheveled strands flop over his forehead. He's also caught the sun and his skin has a beautiful golden tint. *Shit*. I need to stop drooling over Jake. I come back shortly and Jake looks up and smiles at me as I set down the order of drinks and appetizers. I'm wearing my uniform black jeans and his fingers stroke my leg under the table. My heart hiccups, and I smile but don't look at him.

They order more drinks and stay for a long while. The whole time Jake's eyes are on me. One of the guys from the other group I'm serving, writes his phone number on a scrap of paper and folds it, then tucks it into my apron pocket. This kind of thing happens all the time. I'm used to it. These guys get off daring each other to hit on a girl from the staff and it usually just means great tips for Dani and me, so we have fun with it. But as I look up, Jake's eyes are trained on the guy. His jaw is set and he looks like he's about to get up and head over. I make my way to Jake's table and ask them if they're okay on drinks. Jake's eyes lock on mine. He doesn't look happy. I smile and shake my head slightly, letting him know it's not a big deal.

I go back to the bar, and I'm waiting for Zack to fill my next order when Jake appears behind me.

"Everything okay? Are those fuckers being disrespectful?"

"Jake." I smile. "It's no big deal. Guys here do that all the time. It's kind of an Alpha thing to try to get a waitress's attention. It's harmless, and usually means good tips."

Jake nods, but doesn't look any happier.

"It's sweet that you care. But really, it's fine."

He frowns. "Are you going to call him?"

"What?"

"He slipped his number into your apron pocket."

I smile, and reach into my apron, then pull the scrap of paper and hand it to Jake. "Here. You call him." I wink and he stifles a smile, then rolls it into a ball and shoots it behind the bar.

"I woke up and you were gone. Why did you run away?" he mutters so only I can hear. His eyes are liquid brandy. I want to drown in them.

"I didn't run. I wasn't sure how you'd feel about me being there when you woke up. I know we said we would keep things simple." I look down because I'm trying hard to sound unaffected, even though I already know Jake has infiltrated my thoughts and my body in a way that is beginning to scare me. I don't want him infiltrating my heart, too. He tilts my chin up.

"I want to kiss you."

I smile. "You can't. I'm working."

"We'll probably stay in and chill tonight. When can I see you?"

Zack gestures at the waiting order.

"I have to go. But let's figure something out."

"The guys want to swim for an hour after dinner. Come by my villa? Give me your number and I'll text you."

I turn to the bar and load the order on my tray. "I don't have a phone." I give him an apologetic smile. "I sort of threw it against the wall because Marc wouldn't stop calling."

He shakes his head and smiles. "Okay. Come over at eleven. I'll kick them out."

I knock on the door of Jake's villa. It is five after eleven and I hope he managed to get his friends to leave for a while. Going through my shift with Jake so close and not being able to touch him was torture.

The door swings open, and without saying a word he scoops me into his arms and crushes his mouth to mine. He closes the door and pins me behind it. I wrap my legs around his waist and moan when his erection presses against my sex. *Damn*. Fire flares inside me and I can't get enough. I clutch his hair in my fists and turn my head for a breath as his mouth moves to my neck, ravaging me.

"Natalia," he groans, and the delicious sound floods me. "I fucking missed you." He makes quick work of undressing me, and I unbutton and pull his jeans down. He sets me down for a moment to step out of his clothes, and I do the same. I'm panting. My heart bangs against my chest in anticipation. Our eyes meet and our mouths follow. Jake picks me up again and pins me against the door as he thrusts into me. I gasp, and close my eyes to fully absorb the feeling. It's heavenly, and primal, and so incredibly good. I grip his shoulders, and let him fuck me. Slowly, faster, then slow again. He fills me completely, and I surrender. He invades all of me. The glorious scent of leather and sex and Jake infiltrates me once again as I press myself to him.

"Jake. *Damn.*"

He slams deeper into me, and I explode around him. My body trembles. I've lost all command of my limbs. Jake holds me against the door and takes my face in his hands, then kisses me. It's deep and so full of everything. It is as intimate and intense as what we just did. When he pulls away, we are both breathing hard.

"Fuck, Natalia. This is crazy."

"Yeah," I breathe. I feel light headed and drunk with Jake. He kisses me again, then slowly slides me down to my feet and reaches for his clothes. I do the same, and when we're both dressed, he pulls me to the couch with him. I lie sideways with my legs draped over his lap. I yawn. Sex with Jake is exhausting. He smiles.

"Want a drink?"

I shake my head no. "I better go. I have a poker game to win."

"Oh, so I'm down to a booty call?" He grins.

I laugh. "Can I ask you something?"

"Sure."

"How does this work?"

"How does what work?"

"This thing between us. I mean...I hate to think about it because you know my thoughts on the subject, but I can't help feeling like I'm taking advantage of you."

"How so?"

"Well, this...making love to me...it's also sort of...your job, too. How does it work? Are you going to give me a massive bill before you leave?"

He laughs out loud and shakes his head.

"Jake, I'm serious."

"I know. You're killing me, Natalia. Do you seriously think I'll charge you for having sex with you?" He laughs again.

"Um...isn't it what you do *for a living*?"

"Babe. I told you. I'm not that different from every other single guy out there. I fuck whoever I want."

"So I'm *not* getting a bill?"

He chuckles. "No. No bill."

I let out an exaggerated sigh of relief. "Thank God. That would've been one hell of a bill."

At this, he laughs louder. "*That* good, huh?"

"Fucking mind-blowing, Jake." I grin. "Now I have to go." I get up, and he follows me to the door. His arm snakes around my waist and he pulls me into a deep kiss.

"Wanna get some more fucking-mind-blowing sex tomorrow?"

"Cocky smug bastard." I smile.

"The guys are getting up early to hit the slopes. I'll manage to stay back and join them an hour later. Will an hour be enough?"

I reach up and grip his hair at the nape, then kiss him with the same intensity he used on me. "I like your hair."

He grins and threads his fingers through my hair. "I like yours."

"Nine a.m. tomorrow?" I say between kisses.

"I'm already hard."

"Creep."

He grins, and I narrow my eyes, stifling a smile.

I jog back to the lodge, feeling heady and high. It's the Jake effect, and a faint voice from within tells me I'm crossing into dangerous territory. I shut the door on that and hurry to Derek's room to win some more bills for my money pot.

Chapter 18: *Jake*

I close the door and press my forehead against it. *What the hell is happening to me.* This girl is turning into an addiction, and it's getting harder to turn away. Whatever this is, I need to get a fucking handle on it before it gets out of control. I keep trying to prove to myself that the effect she has on me will soon wear off, and I'll be able to breathe again. But it's been the opposite. Every time I see her it's more difficult to say goodbye, then the countdown begins until I see her again. *Fucking Christ.*

I pour myself a drink, racking my brain for some order. If I'm willing to ride this until I leave Aspen in two days, it needs to be my decision. Maybe I can let things play until I leave, and then reevaluate the situation when Natalia and I are apart. In less than two months, we will both be living in the same city and we can keep it going if that's what we want. *Yes.* I'm pleased with my plan, and can now focus on how and where to fuck her.

The guys walk in as I'm stepping out of the shower. They want to call it an early night so we can hit the slopes as soon as they open. I don't tell them about my plan to meet them later in the morning yet. I let them take the bedrooms and offer to take the couch.

In the morning I hear Pete and Dillon rustle around as they eat breakfast. I purposely wait to get off the couch until they're almost ready to go.

"I'm not feeling that hot. Why don't you guys hit the top and I'll catch up with you in an hour or so."

Dillon frowns. "You okay?"

"Yeah." I rub the back of my neck. "I'm just moving a bit slow today."

Pete and I exchange a look and I know he's already called my bullshit act.

"Hope you feel better." He winks and I dart a look at Dillon who's oblivious to my ulterior motives.

It's almost nine when they leave and I'm sweating bullets. I don't want them to run into Natalia on their way out. Luckily a good ten minutes pass before she knocks on the door. When I open it, I'm taken back by her appearance. She's wearing workout clothes and is breathing hard.

"Sorry." She smiles. "I didn't have time for a shower. Wanna do that together?"

Sudden joy fills me. This girl is a constant surprise. I love that about her. Her skin is glowing with sweat and I'm instantly turned on. She smiles at what's happening in my pajama pants, and I wrap her wrist and tug her against me.

"I'm gross, Jake."

I bury my nose in her neck and pick her up as I take a long breath. She laughs, and wraps her legs around me, telling me I'm disgusting and sick, but she's kissing me anyway. I love that she's so comfortable around me, and that the shower together was her idea.

In the bathroom, I strip her clothes off, and pull us under the cascading stream of hot water. She lets me wash her hair, and I'm shocked at how erotic and sensual this simple task is with her. I've done this with other women, but it's never felt this intimate. It was mainly for their pleasure, and didn't mean anything more.

Natalia takes the shampoo and does the same for me. I smile because she's standing on the tips of her toes in order to reach my hair. I lean down to make it easier and she kisses my cheek and says thanks. Unease stirs in my chest at that small gesture, and I need to shake it off. I grab her hips and turn her around so she's facing the wall, then press her to me. She lays her palms against the marble wall and pushes back, slightly bending over. My dick is throbbing, and the need to be inside her takes over. My hands cup her breasts, and she presses against them, arching her head back and pushing her ass against me. I ease into her and she moans out loud. It goes straight to my groin and I push deeper into her.

"Jake. *Damn*."

I slam into her and she grinds back. It doesn't take me long. I come hard inside her, groaning her name as she yells mine, then collapses in my arms.

I turn her around, and cover her mouth with mine. Her lips are soft and wet. She's completely surrendered to me. Her eyes are closed, and her only support is my arm around her waist. She kisses my shoulder and smiles, resting her head on my chest.

"God, what are you doing to me?" she whispers, and I still because that is the same thought that's been roaming in my mind since the first time we met.

"Just making sure you know how good you are at this."

"*This* being..."

"Casual sex. You've mastered the art."

"Oh." She smiles. "That's good to know."

I kiss her, then pull her out of the shower and hold a robe up for her. She looks up at me and hesitates, then slips it on. I don't want her to get dressed just yet because I'm not ready for her to leave.

I make us coffee, and we sit at the dining table in comfortable silence.

"I should probably go," she mutters. Our eyes lock and a quick emotion crosses hers. I wonder if this is as strange for her as it is for me and if she, too, is afraid she'll fall for me.

"What's your schedule like today?" I ask her, downing the last of my coffee. She stifles a smile.

"Um, actually, I have the day off."

I roll my eyes and hang my head. She laughs. This is just my luck. I'm spending the day with two guys and all I'm going to do is think about every minute I could be spending with her.

"When are you free?"

"Well," I say, reaching for her hand and tugging. She stands up and walks toward me. "I'm free right now," I say, then pull on her hand so she sits on my lap, straddling me. I'm already hard. I grip her waist and bring her closer, then untie her robe and slide it off her shoulders. It falls to the floor and my hands move to her breasts. She's naked, and exposed, and mine. My eyes memorize every inch of her. Our eyes lock, and without looking away, I wrap my hands around her knees and spread her legs wider, then lift her up and slide into her. She's wet and ready, and my dick is so hard it hurts.

"Baby," I whisper. "You feel so good."

She grips my shoulders and we start to move. She tilts her head back and closes her eyes as she rides me, moaning every time I push deeper into her.

"Oh, fuck!" she screams and it sends me over. I slam into her, and once again I'm falling into a dark abyss of foreign emotions.

Her arms circle my neck, and she drops her head to my shoulder.

"I think you're trying to kill me," she whispers to my ear. I chuckle.

"Ditto, Princess."

She stills and pulls her head back. "What did you call me?"

I frown. "Princess?" She's suddenly pale. "Baby, what's wrong?"

She shakes her head. "Nothing. It's just...nobody has ever called me that except...Tango. The last time I heard it was two years ago." I cup her face and her eyes are wet. I press a kiss to her lips, and the tears spill down her cheeks.

"I'm sorry."

"It's okay, Jake. Now you know what a head case I am. It's good that you have no expectations because I'm sure I would disappoint you." She watches me for a long moment and doesn't say anything. Her fingers stroke my face, and there's longing in her eyes.

"Jake. What's going to happen after you leave? I mean, we just go our separate ways and that's it?"

I brush the hair off her face. "I think the only thing we can both manage is what's happening right now. But if this is not what you want, we can stop." I'm such an asshole. But it's true. This is all I can manage.

"Do you want to stop?" she murmurs.

I shake my head. "No. Do you?"

"No." She presses her forehead to mine and lets out a long sigh. The darkness stirs in my chest, and there's nothing to hold on to. I wrap my arms around her and squeeze her tight, and she does the same. We stay like that for a long moment, and I wonder if she knows that *she* is what I'm holding on to, because what lies beneath this terrifies me.

Her head rises and she smiles, then gives me a soft kiss and stands up. I watch her walk to the bathroom and retrieve her clothes. She smirks as she slips them on because they're drenched in sweat, but she doesn't have another option if she doesn't want to get caught.

"I should have thought about the 'after,'" she says. "You're messing with my head, Jake." She looks up and winks at me, and I wonder if she knows how much she's been messing with mine.

I dress into my ski clothes and walk her to the door. She grips my shirt at the chest and pulls me for one more kiss.

"What's your last name?"

I frown. "Harper. Yours?"

"Prinz."

I tilt my head and she shrugs. That's probably where the 'Princess' nickname came from.

"You look hot in ski clothes, Jake Harper." She kisses me again and inspiration hits me.

"Come skiing with us."

She stills. "What?"

"Come skiing with us. The guys won't mind and it'll be fun."

"Jake. I don't know if…" She smiles and I grin back.

"You don't know if it's a good idea."

She stifles a smile and I kiss her.

"Come on," I say against her mouth. "Meet us at Spyglass for lunch."

"Are you sure? You should spend time with your friends."

"Pete, Dillon and I go on ski trips all the time. They won't care."

"Okay." She smiles.

"Okay."

It's one o'clock when we finally make it to the Spyglass lounge. It's swarming with people and I'm scanning the room for Natalia. I've already told the guys she'd be joining us. Dillon seemed fine with it, and Pete was even excited. I wish he'd stop busting my balls over it. I'm not going to fucking marry the girl.

She's sitting by the window at a table big enough for all of us. She looks up and smiles when our eyes meet. The guys slump into the seats and I lean down to kiss her. She tenses, then goes with it and relaxes.

During lunch, Pete and Dillon grill Natalia with questions about the mountain. I'm impressed at how well she knows it. She tells them about some virgin trails at the back where there's sure to be fresh powder. It requires some hiking, but if we're game she can lead us to them. The guys are thrilled. Pete keeps sending me pointed looks. I give him a warning glare.

Once we are finished with lunch, we dress back into our gear and follow Natalia to the back of the mountain. She's fun to ski with and can easily keep up with Pete and Dillon, who are exceptional skiers. She blazes down the runs as if she's weightless. We traverse across a slim path at the summit that will take us to the virgin trails she mentioned. She's leading us and I stay close behind. Watching her ski so close to the drop-off on the other side is making me uneasy, and my protective instinct kicks in.

We finally make it to the end of the trail, and she points down. I take a minute to watch the view. It's spectacular, and we are the only skiers here. I slide down to where Natalia is and lean down to kiss her.

"It makes me nervous having you up here. Will you promise to take it easy? I saw the way you took those turns back there."

She smiles. "I'll be fine, Jake."

"Promise me," I say against her lips.

"Okay," she whispers. "You worry too much, Jake Harper." She kisses me chastely, then turns, and before I can blink, she's pushed herself off the edge and is flying down through the powder. Dillon whistles and jumps after her, then Pete slides down and stops by me.

"What a girl." He winks, and before I can punch him, he's off after them.

I lower my goggles and slide off, fighting the tightness in my chest until I see she's safe again.

Back at the base, Natalia pulls her helmet and goggles off, letting down that wild mane of sable hair. Several heads turn around and I groan inwardly, because a group of guys is now checking her out. She looks up at me and her face is glowing. I cut the distance between us, and before she can react, I wrap my arm around her and pull her into a kiss. Her lips are cold as they part to welcome my tongue. Then she quickly pulls away.

"Jake. Not here." She grimaces.

"I'm sorry," I say, even though I'm not sorry at all. I narrow my eyes. "You promised me you'd slow down."

"Oops." She smiles.

"We are going into town for dinner. Come?"

Her eyebrows shoot up. Fuck. I sound clingy. But I don't give a shit.

"Come on."

"Jake, this is your guys trip." She glances at Dillon and Pete who are already heading to the lounge for a beer.

"They won't care if you're there."

"Of course, they care. They're just being nice."

"Come."

"How about I meet you afterwards for a drink?"

I look at her for a long moment. I want her to come with us, but I also like that she respects my time with the guys. I tell her

Dani has my number and ask her to call me at around nine in the evening. She smiles and says okay.

At the lounge, the guys are already on their second beer. Dillon grills me with questions about Natalia, but I keep it vague. Pete shakes his head and smiles, and I know he'll grill me later without Dillon around. Dillon's eyes are now trained on Dani, who's sliding the beers onto the table. He takes every opportunity to flirt with her and before we leave, he tells her Natalia is meeting us for drinks later and asks her to join us. She looks up at him and smiles, and I already know this is a runaway train. I shake my head because Natalia would think *this is not a good idea.*

Chapter 19: *Natalia*:

Dani barges into our room as I'm coming out of the shower. She has a wicked grin on her face. I narrow my eyes.

"What?"

"Got myself a date with a pretty hot guy."

I nod, relieved, and head to the closet. The fact that Dani has a date with a hot guy is not news. Sometimes I envy her lack of depth when it comes to relationships with guys. She has a great time, then gets on with her life.

"Where are you going?" I ask, annoyed at the lack of choices in my wardrobe.

"Same place you are. My date is with Dillon."

I whip my head around and she grins.

"Dani. No. Why him?"

"Why *not* him?"

"Dani, things with Jake are already weird enough as they are. Do you think getting involved with his friend is a good idea?"

"Yes. He's cute. Besides, they're both leaving the day after tomorrow, so no strings attached, Nati," she says, pulling off her sneakers. "Let's just have a good time. When was the last time you and I went out on a double date?"

I shrug.

"Come on. It'll be fun. Besides, I think you need this." She squeezes my shoulder and leaves to the shower. I plop down on my bed, staring at the ceiling. I guess she's right. It's not like Jake and I are planning to see each other at all after he leaves.

The thought depresses me.

I close my eyes. My head is a knot of confusion. There are moments when I miss Marc. So many memories barge unbidden in my head at the oddest times, leaving a sense of emptiness in their wake. Then I get angry. Angry at Marc for cheating, at me for trusting him so blindly, and at life for once again taking away someone I loved.

But lately, I'm also overpowered by thoughts of Jake and the new memories we made together in the short time that I've known him. The swimming lessons, the day he found me in the snow, our shower together this morning. Damn, that was hot.

But the more I think about what Jake and I are doing, the more I know this whole 'in the moment thing' is a ticking bomb that will eventually blow up in my face. Jake is quickly penetrating through the armor I've built around my heart since Tango died. And that scares the living shit out of me.

Because I already know how this story ends.

Downtown Aspen is swarming with the après-ski crowd. The bar where we are meeting the guys is a casual place in the style of an old wood cabin. There is a pool table surrounded by booths and a stage adjacent to a dance floor where a live band is playing classic rock covers. The atmosphere is fun and lively.

Jake is sitting at a booth across from Dillon and Pete. When I approach, he stands up to let me in and greets me with a kiss. Pete slides out to let Dani sit next to Dillon, who appraises her with a wide smile.

We order beers and reminisce about the day's skiing. The guys seem impressed with the little tour I gave them down the back of the mountain and say they want to go back tomorrow. Dani and I have the day off and the guys insist we go skiing with them. We discuss possible routes and the whole time Jake's hand is stroking my knee under the table. When I look up at him, he leans over and gives me a sensual kiss on the neck.

"You smell good. I still have images of you in my shower. It's driving me crazy," he whispers in my ear. I blush scarlet, and Dani gives me a knowing look from across the table. Dillon's eyes meet mine and he smiles, then he looks at Jake with a puzzled expression that makes me think Jake probably doesn't normally act this way around him. Or maybe I'm just hoping. I interlace my fingers with Jake's and he kisses my knuckles.

"Dance with me."

It's like he's talking directly to my libido. I have to squeeze my knees together to brace the shot of lust that swirls between my legs. I slide out of the booth, and Jake takes my hand to lead me to the dance floor. There is a slow melody playing, and he pulls me against him, enveloping me in his arms. I close my eyes and lean my head on his shoulder. Part of me surrenders, and part of me wants to stop what this is doing to me, the physical closeness to his body. But he starts kissing my neck and I melt.

"Jake."

"I can't stop thinking about you, naked on my lap," he whispers, and I nearly expire. He pulls away so our eyes meet, then lowers his mouth to mine and kisses me slowly, tenderly, his arms squeezing me so hard against his chest I'm not sure I can breathe. The kiss deepens and I fall into the abyss that is Jake, a place where I only have the present. I decide to take everything he's willing to give me and kiss him with the same abandon, losing myself in the now.

When we break the kiss, we're panting. Jake presses his forehead to mine and lets out a long sigh, but says nothing as we move slowly to the music.

A few minutes later, the singer says they'll take a short break, and we return to our table. Pete, Dillon and Dani are playing pool a few feet away. We watch them as we sip on our beers. Jake is very quiet and I'm not sure if it's the funky mood I'm in tonight, or if he's having similar thoughts about what will happen with us after he leaves.

We join the pool game, and for the next hour, I forget about the fact that my minutes with Jake are counted. Pete is a good player. I like the way he interacts with Jake. I can tell they've been friends for a long time. Pete teases him and Jake doesn't seem to mind. Meanwhile, Dillon and Dani can't take their hands off each other. He wraps himself around her whenever it's her turn to shoot and looks thrilled that she can still make a straight shot. Pete and Jake exchange looks and taunt Dillon.

The guys and Dani play another game with newcomers that want to up the stakes by making bets. Jake and I go back to the table to finish our beers. He tugs on my hand and slides me onto his lap.

"Stay the night with me," he says against my mouth. "I want to spend as much time with you as I can before I leave."

"Jake. Your friends? I can't come over."

"Maybe I come over to you."

I chuckle. "Dani would love that. And I'm not joking."

"Actually, Dillon said Dani is spending the night with him."

I whip my head around and raise my eyebrows. That's a little too fast, even for Dani. Jake shrugs.

"They've already discussed it." He smiles.

I look at Dani and frown, shaking my head. Jake wraps his arms around my waist and rests his chin on my shoulder.

"Don't give her a hard time. I need this. And so do you," he says to my ear, sending chills up my back. I smile because he's right. As much as spending every free minute I have with Jake scares me, I know I want all the time I can get with him. I turn on his lap and kiss him, letting him know how much I want this, too. He tells me he's hard and it makes me smile. I like that I can do that to him. His hand slips under my sweater and he strokes my stomach with his thumb. We stay like that, watching the pool game and pretending we're not falling hard.

Chapter 20: *Jake*

I open my eyes in the dim light of Natalia's room, then close them again. Images from last night flood my thoughts. The stop at the Crêpe Wagon on the way back because she had skipped dinner and was famished. The wind had died down and the snow drifted in overweight snowflakes. She kissed the corner of my mouth, and told me I went well with chocolate. Then our sneaking around the back of the resort, her laughter when we both tripped and fell face down in the snow; our race to take each other's clothes off in her room. Then sex. So much fucking incredible sex.

The alarm clock says it's six in the morning. I fight the urge to wake her up and pull her into the shower with me. But the hotel staff will soon start circulating, and I need to leave before I'm seen walking out of her room or through the employee hallway. I already feel bad about leaving tomorrow, and giving her no prospects of a future visit. I don't want to screw up things at work for her, too.

I watch her sleep as I dress. She looks beautiful, her hair masterfully ruffled over her shoulders and naked back. She's lying on her front, the comforter halfway down her waist, exposing her perfect skin. I want to lean over and kiss every inch of her, but I refrain. Instead, I leave her a note and quietly sneak out.

I make my way to the back of the property and into my villa, feeling every inch the asshole that I am. Natalia was quiet yesterday, and I recognized the dominating emotion in her eyes: longing. Or maybe regret. Maybe she wishes we hadn't crossed that invisible line. She walked right through it, and what scares me the most, is that I did, too.

Yesterday I considered extending my stay, but as I step through the early morning snow, I'm convinced that the only way to get a handle on things is by putting physical distance between us. I need to go back to L.A. as I planned. Maybe I can let a few weeks go by, then come and visit her if I want. Who am I kidding. I already know I will.

The cabin is quiet when I slip in. I get the coffee machine going, then sink on the couch while I wait. Pete's door opens a few minutes later and he shuffles out, half asleep. He greets me with a nod, and when I get up, he's at the table with two cups of coffee.

"Rough night?" he mumbles, taking in my not-so-rested-appearance.

I ignore him and take a sip of black poison. Pete makes the strongest damn coffee I've ever tasted. He says it's his way to tackle the day head first.

His eyes are still on me, and I can already hear a speech coming. I don't want to deal with one of his fucking speeches today.

"Pete, I know you've imagined my whole future already, but things with Natalia are not what you think they are. We have an understanding and that's that."

"Is that right?"

"Yeah." I lock eyes with him. "My life's on track. I decide what happens next and I'm happy with things as they are. I don't need complications."

He chuckles. "Seriously, Jake? Are you listening to yourself? Because that's the biggest load of bullshit I've heard you say in a long time."

I glare at him, but he doesn't flinch. The other thing about Pete is that he's the most persistent motherfucker I've ever known. When he gets an idea in his head about the way things should be he doesn't let up. We've gotten into arguments before in which at least one of us ended up with a black eye. I've always sort of respected that about him, but right now he's pissing me off.

"I need to get a hold on things. I need to go back to Santa Monica and start working on the move and what I need to do for the shop. It's not a good time for distractions."

"She's a distraction, alright," he mutters. "She's smart as fuck, beautiful, and for some damn reason I don't yet understand, she's falling for you, even though she's well aware of what you do for a living. Come on, Jake. You and I know girls like her are not around for long. Some other lucky fucker is going to push you out of the race if you don't get your shit together. "

"Goddammit, Pete. Let it the fuck go. There's nothing more than sex between Natalia and me. She's getting over her ex, and I'm...I don't even know what the hell I'm doing anymore. And that's why I need to fuck off and go back to L.A."

Pete stands up and runs a hand through his hair. "Whatever, man."

Dillon walks out of his room looking no more rested than me. He glances over at the two of us, and his mouth stretches into a grin.

"Morning, fellas."

Pete rolls his eyes. "You, asshole, could've been more considerate of the fact that there is only one wall between your bedroom and mine."

Dillon's grin widens. "Jealous? Is married sex already boring for you, Pete? I wouldn't have guessed. Syd's hot."

With a whiplash move, Pete grips Dillon into a headlock and grins. "That's my wife you're talking about, asshole. Give her the respect she deserves."

Dillon tries to break lose, but Pete has him. He finally lets go.

"And yeah. She is hot. But only I get to say that."

Dillon flexes his neck, and smiles while he pours himself coffee. He and Pete have known each other since they were kids and wrestling has always been a big part of their problem-solving with each other.

Dani walks out of Dillon's room wearing her clothes from last night. Despite the early hour, she's a very pretty girl. I get why Dillon is shitfaced about her. He looks at her and his eyes light up. I'm surprised she's still here because Dillon never lets girls sleep over, but then, she couldn't go back to her room with me there. Or maybe these Argentinean women put a spell on us.

She slides onto his lap and I expect him to find an excuse to move her off, but he wraps his arms around her and pulls her into a kiss.

I'll be damned.

We make plans to meet up top in an hour. Pete, Dillon and I leave first and Dani says she will go change, then she and Natalia will join us at Needles.

At the summit, the guys and I race each other through the fresh powder. My legs are burning and I welcome the distraction from whatever is going on in my chest.

When the girls meet up with us, Natalia's eyes are blazing emeralds. She kisses Pete and Dillon's cheeks, then looks at me and smiles. I slide over to her as she clips her skis on, then lean down to kiss her.

"Morning," I mutter. She smells amazing. I want to bail on the skiing and take her back to bed.

"Hi, Jake." Those eyes lock into mine. *Christ.* "Let's have fun." She lowers her goggles, then pushes off her poles and slides toward the guys and Dani who are waiting by the edge of a trail. She pauses beside them, then disappears downhill.

I clench my teeth and follow the group, who is taking turns slicing the mountain behind Natalia. And I know the next twenty four hours will be a fucking war. What I'm not sure of, is if the war will be between Natalia and me, or the two sides of me who will not come to an agreement over what will happen next.

Chapter 21: *Natalia*:

By the time we call it a day, it's past four. My legs are practically shaking from the exertion of a long ski day. It feels good and it temporarily distracts my thoughts from constantly going back to Jake.

Jake who taught me how to swim.

Jake who saved me from dying in the snow.

Jake who is leaving tomorrow.

At the base of the mountain, Dani circles her arms around Dillon's neck. I can't wait to get her alone. I have never seen Dani this clingy with a guy. In her defense, Dillon looks equally whipped. Or maybe all American men are masters at making women believe they're interested. The jury's still out on that one.

Jake props his skis on one shoulder and walks to where I am. I'm forcing my eyes to focus on anything but him because he looks like he just walked out of a catalog for ski apparel.

We've played a cat and mouse game all day, and I'm mainly responsible for that. I just don't know how to feign disinterest, when all I want is for him to stay longer. I shake my head. Now I'm being ridiculous. Jake is not attached to anyone and I'd be a fool to think 'I can change him.' I want to slap myself and throw me under a cold shower.

He approaches, and I can feel his eyes burning on me. I look up and our eyes lock. In the glow of the snow his eyes have that endless brandy hue that makes my brain forget its basic functions.

"Want to hang out later?" He smiles. "It's our last night."

Now I want to slap *him*, because I don't need any reminders that this will be our last night together. Jesus, it would probably be a good idea for me to spend the night by myself, away from any sharp objects.

"Sure," I murmur, because despite the violent thoughts, I'm a fool and I want every minute he can give me.

"Dani said there's a party later in the village for somebody's birthday? Do you think the guys and I can come?"

I nod.

"What's the matter?" He frowns.

I don't want you to go. "Nothing. I'm just spent."

He wraps me in his arms. His frame towers over me and I press my face against his jacket. It's cold. Like me. I bite hard to rein in the tears. My throat swells until it hurts.

"Maybe we can sneak out early and come back to my villa," he whispers in my ear. "I want to spend time alone with you." He pulls back and brushes my cheek with the back of his hand. It's getting damn hard not to cry. Reaching up, I close my eyes and kiss him.

"That sounds great."

Dani, Zack, and I order drinks at the sports bar where Lane's party takes place. It didn't start until nine in the evening, and the day staff from the resort trickles in as they finish their shifts. The party will go until sunrise, and tomorrow everyone will walk around like zombies. It suits me just fine, because I already want to erase tomorrow.

Jake and his friends will be meeting us here at some point. For the moment, I enjoy time alone with my two friends. I spent the first ten minutes grilling Dani over Dillon. She has no defense. She's totally into him, and that's that. I have never seen Dani so 'into' someone. I shake my head and look at Zack. He's been quiet and has a somber halo over his head. I kick him under the table to get his attention.

"What's the matter? It's a party." *Huh*. He could be saying the exact same thing to me.

"Mariana broke up with me. Over the fucking phone." His eyes are trained on his beer.

"What the fuck. Seriously? Why?" Dani and I look at each other. She shakes her head slightly to let me know this is news to her, too.

He shrugs. "She can't handle the long distance, I guess."

"Zack, you're going home in a *month*." I frown.

"I underestimated the whole long distance thing," he says, still looking at the beer as if it contains the dreams he just lost. "I thought we could do it."

"Jesus, Zack." I reach over the table for his hand and squeeze it. "You and me. We both did. But that doesn't change that Marc and Mariana are a pair of assholes for letting us believe everything was all right. Marc and Mariana." I smirk. "They even sound like a couple of fuckers."

Zack chuckles. "Yeah. I guess she met someone else, too."

I roll my eyes. "*Shit*. Of course."

Zack finally looks up from his beer. His eyes are etched with hurt. He doesn't deserve this. *Fuckdammit.* I stand up and take Zack's hand. "Come here." He obeys and I pull him into a hug. At first his arms are limp, then they slowly circle around my back and hug me. I tighten mine and after a few seconds his grip is so tight I can barely breathe. I close my eyes and the tears spill down my cheeks. I'm not sure if I'm crying just for Zack, or for me as well.

He finally pulls away and I quickly wipe my cheeks. He rubs my head when he sees my eyes wet.

"Let's get shitfaced." He forces a grin and I nod. Dani locks eyes with Zack and she blows him a kiss as he sits down. He smiles.

Jake, Pete and Dillon are suddenly at the table. I didn't hear them approach at all. When I look up at Jake he's scowling. His eyes dart from Zack to mine. What's his problem? Dillon pulls Dani into his arms and gives her a deep kiss. I feel a pang of jealousy. Dani doesn't seem affected by the fact that Dillon is leaving tomorrow. I wish I could be as 'in the moment' as Dani.

The guys slide into the long booth. Before sitting down, Jake tugs on my hand and leans down to kiss me.

"Everything okay?" he whispers. His eyes Dart to Zack, who is talking to Pete.

"Yup."

He nods and slides into the seat beside me.

We have a few beers, and after a couple of hours, it's hard to keep my eyes open. Dani and Dillon have already disappeared. Pete is engaged in a pool game with Zack, Derek and other guys from the resort. Jake and I are the only ones left at our table. Neither of us has said much tonight, and I'm overpowered by a sense of dread.

"Do you mind if we leave?" I look up at Jake and he gives me a half-smile.

"Of course not. Let me just tell Pete."

I watch him while he makes his way to where Pete is and they have a brief conversation. Pete pats his back and says something that makes Jake shake his head in annoyance. I want to know what Pete said.

Sneaking into my room is easy, since most of the day staff is at the party, and the night shift is in the guest areas. As soon as I close the door behind us, Jake pulls me into his arms and kisses me hard. I close my eyes and try not to think that I won't get to do this with him after tonight. I won't be able to touch him. The thought burns as it whirls inside my head. I kiss him back hard, so hard he has to grip my shoulders and pull me back so he can take a breath. Our eyes meet and it's too late.

I'm already crying.

"Don't," he mutters. His eyes are drawn in pain.

"Sorry." My voice is raspy and thick with emotion.

He hugs me tight and we stay like that for a long time. Just holding each other. Then he takes my face in his hands and kisses me deeply. I tangle my fingers in his hair and do the same. Our tongues intertwine in a sensual dance. We undress each other. Slowly at first, then with movements that become more and more desperate. We drop on the bed, our mouths saying all the things our words can't.

Jake presses me down to the mattress, my body pinned under his weight, then thrusts inside me almost violently. I gasp, not from pain, but surprise. He fills me completely and it's heaven. He presses himself deeper, then pulls back, then does it again. His fingers brush the hair off my face. His eyes are blazing as they lock into mine.

"Tell me something," he says. His voice is hoarse with need. "What will you do tomorrow? Will you think of me?" He thrusts deeper and I gasp. "Tell me," he whispers.

I blink at him. It is hard to focus on anything, but the amazing feeling of him inside me. I want to close my eyes and let go, but his eyes are so intense it's impossible to look away.

"Tomorrow...doesn't matter, Jake. You'll be gone."

He thrusts into me again and I close my eyes, but he holds my chin with his hand.

"Will you be with him?"

I frown. "What? Who?" I'm breathless. He possesses all of me and I want to surrender.

"Your friend. I saw you in his arms, tonight."

What? WTF? The inebriating lust from a second ago recedes like a whip. Pressing my hands against his chest, I push him off me. I wince when he pulls out of me and sits back. My whole body tenses in protest. Jake frowns and watches me as I slide against the headboard.

"What the hell, Jake?" I mutter. "What gives you the right to ask me that? Even if you saw what you think you saw?"

He closes his eyes as if he's reining in his temper.

"Nothing. I have no right. I just...*dammit*, Natalia. I can't let go of you."

"Why?"

"I don't know," he snaps. "I've been trying to figure out the same thing since I first met you. *Fuck*. We've been through this. I don't get involved with women this way."

His words cut through me and the reminder of the way in which he does get involved with women seeps into me like poison.

"Why is that, Jake?"

"Natalia." He lets out a deep sigh. "Let's not do this now."

I ignore the bewitching sound of my name as it travels through me. "I want to know, Jake."

"Don't." He frowns.

I frown back and neither of us says anything more. Our eyes are locked in a stupid stare-off. He's sitting at the foot of the bed and I'm pressed against the headboard. The air between us is electric.

The seconds pass, melting away the little time we have left together. My heart constricts. I don't want to argue. I want to be pressed against him, so tight that there is no space at all between our bodies.

Jake closes his eyes and hangs his head in resignation, and I think he's about to get up and leave. Panic flashes through me and

I launch myself to him, wrapping my legs and arms around his body like a vine.

"Let's go back to before this conversation started." I say against his mouth. "Let's not talk anymore tonight, Jake." I crush my mouth against his, and after a second, his arms are around me and he's lowering me back onto the bed. I'm immediately aroused and he groans when his hand moves between my legs and his fingers slide in and out of me.

"Fuck," he whispers, and then he's inside me. It's desperate, guttural, and driven by need. I match his every move because in this moment we are both feeling the same. He slams into me and I'm lost, drunk with images of Jake as the rest of the world fades.

That night I don't move to Dani's bed. I stay in Jake's arms, letting his scent intoxicate me. It's permanently imprinted in my memory. Maybe if I breathe it for a whole night it will last me after he's gone.

Chapter 22: *Jake*

I unlock my apartment and drop my bags by the door. The last few hours disappeared in a blur. When I woke up this morning, a sense of absolute peace filled me. I breathed it in and out. Natalia lay asleep in my arms, her warmth and mine blended into one. Then consciousness drifted in, and the rusted darkness within me rose to the surface, erasing the last of the peace. My heart fist punched my chest. I was sure she would wake from the pounding.

I untangled myself from her body, careful not to wake her, and picked up my clothes in haste, driven by the desperation that possessed me. Gripping the doorknob I paused to take one last look. She was beautiful, a mystical siren lost in her dreams. Her hair cascaded down her back in unruly sable strands that brushed the sheet hugging her waist. I knew I was being a coward by running away like that. She would miss me when she woke. But the war that exploded inside me could not be put into words. *What have you started?* I thought. And I needed to strip those feelings off like a bandage if I wanted to keep the darkness locked.

There was no other way.

I sink into the couch watching the marine layer fog the floor to ceiling windows of my apartment. This used to be my haven, my safe place. No women here.

No past.

Just me.

But the unease gripping my chest won't give. Natalia filtered in through the old scars of my heart. Scars that have been there since I was eight years old.

An image of Natalia crying last night flashes in my mind and the fist in my chest rattles. *You fucking prick. You are hollow, Jake. You pathetic fuck.* I roam around the room like a caged animal, then turn the stereo up loud. The Foo Fighters momentarily drown the silence that used to comfort me, but they fail to drown the noise in my head.

I pour myself a scotch and down it. Another. Then another. By the fourth one the hole in my chest is replaced by numbness. My phone rings persistently. It's the fourth time since I've landed, but I don't bother. I know it's Tamara, or one of the others. *The others that pay the bills, asshole.* I don't even check my messages. I pour myself another drink and welcome the numbness.

Bleaching morning light echoes against the stark white walls of my apartment. I use to like the simplicity of it. Nothing to disturb the perfect environment I exist in. Now it seems surgical, calculated, and cold. *Wasn't that the point? To not feel?* I close my eyes, and memories from Natalia bleed into my mind in Scorsese-red. I force myself up and slip into shorts and running shoes, then bolt into a run along the beach. The marine layer is thick, moisture beading my face and bare torso as I push my muscles into exertion. My head is still foggy from the alcohol and lack of food. I pass the Santa Monica Pier, then Muscle Beach. It's all bleak at this early hour, the skeleton of a pulsing body that will later come to life.

Now it's only me and the piercing chant of the seagulls as they hover around leftovers and rotting seaweed.

By the time I get back home, I can't think. I simply exist. That's what I love about physical exercise. At some point exertion takes over the brain.

I shower and quickly scan through my messages as I wait for my coffee to brew. Two from Tamara and two more from clients I booked for later this month. They want to confirm trips, parties and all the events that normally fill my life. Now, having to follow through with the plans I made seems like a sentence. I don't really need the money anymore. I've saved enough. *Then why do you do it, Jake?* Natalia's voice torments me. *Everyone deserves to be loved.*

I open my laptop and dive into the list I made for the surf shop. I have vendors to visit this month. I'm momentarily distracted by the ideas I have for the design and a flicker of excitement snaps somewhere inside my ribcage. For the next two hours, I get lost in the tasks that I need to accomplish to make this dream happen.

The week comes and goes. I purposely fill every hour so I can keep a good grip on my mind. Natalia still manages to trespass my thoughts. Alcohol is a good antidote, and it makes the idea of the upcoming trips and time with my clients more bearable.

Dillon calls me to tell me he's going back to Aspen to see Dani. He wants me to go with him, but I tell him I can't.

I know that when Natalia sees Dillon show up alone it will hurt her. I curse myself for hurting her even when I'm not there to do it in person. Fuck my obsession to prove myself wrong. That's what started all this. She wasn't like the others. I know that now. Natalia isn't like anyone.

Thursday, I fly to New York to meet Tamara. She's booked me for a quick trip until Sunday for some events she needs to attend. She's now talking to some big wig from the Museum of Modern Art. We are at a party in his penthouse overlooking Park Avenue. I tune out of the conversation and sip my scotch. Tamara is a pro. She laughs at all the right moments. It's all staged. Thousands of dollars have been spent at this charity event to persuade these people to, in turn, donate their money for a good cause. It's all a circus where the animals scratch each other's back at the right angles.

Tamara turns to me and smiles. We are alone and she snakes her arm around my waist. I don't feel anything, as usual, but smile back at her. She's paid for it.

"You look stunning in a tux, Jake. Do you want to go? I think I want to have you all for myself now."

I give her a brief nod, fighting the sudden urge to rip this monkey suit off me and run to the airport.

Later that night, I watch Manhattan from Tamara's penthouse on the Upper West Side while she sleeps. Tamara likes expensive things. Only the best. She can afford it as the marketing head of a pharmaceutical company. In Tamara's life, every minute is gold. That's why her only relationship is one she pays for. No time for complications or tangled emotions. Everything is simpler in black and white.

The city lights glimmer in the distance and behind the thick glass of the floor to ceiling window, I feel like a caged animal.

Maybe it's time for a change.

I resent the thought. I used to feel like the luckiest bastard on earth. Being flown around the world by wealthy women who paid my weight in gold just to have me show up with them at a party. Well...maybe not *just* that. But it's never been only the money. All the while, being able to keep my interactions with women at bay brought an incredible rush. I'd been dealt a shitty hand early in life, and now I was beating the game, big time. As long as I was winning I was ahead at the game that promised no stabs to the heart. No exchanges, except for money and pleasure. And I've always been good at winning.

Until now.

For the first time, I'm out of my comfort zone. I feel the pull back to Aspen. Back to that girl with untamed black hair and fierce green eyes. I know there is now hurt in those eyes. I know, because I put it there. *Bastard*. I should get a medal.

I pour myself a scotch and down it, then lie down next to Tamara, who's been asleep for a while now. I close my eyes and feel the frost rise from within. I pull the covers over me, but they do nothing to warm me up. I crave the warmth that always radiated from Natalia. Tamara's body is not warm like hers. I wonder why that is.

In the morning, we visit a few art galleries and Tamara buys a piece for her home in the Hamptons. We have a party the day after tomorrow with some moguls from her company's competition.

Another party.

We have lunch, then go back to her place. I fuck her with automated motion, and she can tell something's up.

"What's wrong?" she asks. Tamara never asks any questions, so this throws me off.

"Nothing," I say almost immediately. I curse myself for letting my emotions slip. She accepts my lack of an answer the way she always does and tells me she wants to go shopping.

We visit a few boutiques, and I give her my opinion on the dresses she tries on for the party. As the day advances, dread and hollowness fill me. By the time we're back at her penthouse, it's unbearable.

"Let's order food in," she says as she walks out of the shower. "I don't feel like going out."

I stare through the window at the park below. My hands close into fists. The grip on my chest tightens.

"Tamara." I turn around to face her. "I need to go back to Santa Monica, tonight."

She frowns. "What? Why?"

"There's something urgent I need to take care of." I walk toward her and brush her face with the back of my hand. "I'm sorry, babe. Ryan is available to go to the party, if you want."

She watches me for a moment. I know she will like Ryan. We met at a party a while back. He's new to the business, and when I called him ten minutes ago he jumped at the opportunity to go on a date with Tamara.

"Is everything alright, Jake?" For the second time today, she attempts to step into my personal world. I don't like it. That's one of the reasons all my clients are on the East Coast, as far as possible from my own life.

"Everything's fine." I kiss her forehead. "I have a flight booked from JFK in two hours."

"Jake," she says before can I turn around to pack my bag. I have never walked out on a job before, and Tamara is not the kind of woman you walk out on. I expect some kind of a scene. But she just looks at me with a strange emotion in her eyes. "You take care."

Chapter 23: *Natalia*

Dani and I go about our day as if Jake and Dillon never happened. Dani acts the same way she always does, but I know better. She's serene, reigned in from her usual explosive self. She doesn't talk much to the customers either, doesn't make jokes about them. No snarky comments that make me laugh hard or gape in horror. Nothing. Just plain'ol Dani, if there's such a thing.

She cares about Dillon.

I care about Jake.

We are two fools swimming in a pool of sweet memories that left a sour taste.

She never mentions Dillon and I don't ask. But when I get up from the computer to go to bed one night, she walks out of the bathroom and tugs me into a hug. We don't say anything. We just hug. And I know she's hurting.

On Friday, the lounge is swarming with the après-ski crowd. It's all back to normal. Groups of guys flirting with us and tucking their numbers into our pockets. Too-blonde girls with perfect manicures, shaking the snowflakes off their expensive ski gear as they walk in.

Dani, Zack, and I, are making bets on table seven. Who's going home with whom. The tips are rolling thick, and it looks like a profitable evening for the three of us.

Dani and I wait at the bar while Zack fills our drink orders. She's laughing at the scrap of paper she just pulled from her pocket and reads it out loud *'Call me. I'll be your slave for a night.'*

"I'll never understand these guys' hard-ons for waitresses." I chuckle. Dani laughs again, then her expression freezes as her eyes rise to the far entrance.

"Holy shit," she breathes.

My eyes follow her as she bolts in that direction, then I freeze, too. Dillon drops a duffel bag by his side and extends his arms in welcome. A megawatt smile stretches his mouth as Dani launches herself into his arms.

My heart stills and I hold my breath while my eyes scan the space around him.

Empty.

I wait, and wait, and wait, and as the seconds fade, so does the spark of hope I felt.

He's not here.

I immediately feel like a fool. Hope was never something Jake offered me. Zack must see the hurt in my expression because he gently squeezes my elbow and gives me a half-smile.

"Ready," he says, gesturing to the drinks on my tray. I nod and turn away from Dani and Dillon and the sudden tornado of memories that just ravaged my mind.

I don't see Dani all weekend. She switched her days off with another girl and disappeared with Dillon to the cabin he rented outside the property. I'm happy for her, and it's strange that her happiness also hurts. I shake off the selfish thought, dreading the few weeks I have left at the resort. In less than a month, I'll be in San Diego starting the life I've been crafting for myself all these years.

Minus one lying, cheating fiancé.

As soon as my shift ends I slip into my swimsuit and throw on sweats and a long sleeve shirt under a robe. The night is below freezing, and even though I don't feel like swimming, I go anyway because the alternatives are a washed-out poker game with the guys, or hanging out in my room. Besides, I haven't practiced since Jake left. I already know that goddamn pool will remind me of him, but I have three weeks to get my shit together, so I girl-up and go.

I make a slow journey along the hallway that leads to the pool. It's past eleven, and even from where I am, I can see it's empty. The freezing weather has chased away the regulars that swim laps.

As I push the door the whole area comes into view. My eyes instinctively dart to the jacuzzi.

That's when I see him.

I am stunned, but my feet are making their way toward him like he's a magnet and I'm a scrap of metal. I can't stop. Part of me wants to. A very small part. But I know I can't.

He watches me approach with a guarded expression. He's submerged all the way to his neck, then his shoulders rise as I stop next to him. He never takes his eyes off of me.

God, he's beautiful.

His hair is still dry, a ruffled mess in perfect disarray. I curl my fingers inside the pockets of my robe and let the silence between us thicken.

"How's the swimming coming?" He says it as if he's just left me on my own to practice for ten minutes, and is now coming back to check. I strangle all the emotions rising from my chest and keep my expression stoic.

"Why are you here?" I mutter. It's almost a whisper, but I don't care why he's here. He came back.

"I can't stay away," he says matter-of-factly. His mouth is grim, as if the words burned on their way out, but his eyes are full of everything.

"Natalia."

I close my eyes and hang my head as the sound travels through every single part of me. I hear him emerge from the water, but keep my eyes closed. His feet pad on the wet tiles, and even though I can't see him, I feel the heat that radiates from him. It's almost unbearable.

He has to be fucking freezing, but he ignores it and wraps his arms around me in a death grip. Everything inside me tenses and comes to a halt. I'm in a sensory overload. His smell, his heat, the wet skin of his chest against my chilled face.

I don't move. I can't.

"God, I've missed you. Can we talk inside?" he says in a low voice.

The words are stuck in my throat, so I nod. When he withdraws, the arctic air slaps me. It's a warning, I think. Because I know whatever this is, it's going to hurt later.

He shrugs his robe on and I follow him to the villa he rented. Our hands hang close, but we don't touch. It's hard enough to be this close to him.

He lets me in, then closes the door and reaches for my hand. The static between our fingers sizzles and I pull mine away. He curls his fingers in and lets out a small sigh. He then sits on the couch, extending his hand in an invitation. I look at his hand for a long moment. This is my last chance to run. I'm entitled to it after the way he left the last time.

But I don't.

I sit on the corner of the couch as far away from him as possible. He nods once like he understands.

"Why did you leave like that Jake?" The words are out before I realize. He winces as if I just slapped him.

"This...you...I don't know how to do this."

"Then don't. Why keep coming back?" I say acidly.

He nods, then those stunning eyes meet mine. My fortress crumbles at the corner.

"I can't stay away."

"Then what?"

His eyebrows meet. He looks as if I just asked him to tell me what the weather is on Mars.

"I don't know, Natalia. I just...I needed to see you."

The way he says that, *needed*, rips the stitches in my still fresh wound.

"Jake, I can't. I'm sorry. I just...can't." I stand and head for the door. He beats me to it and presses his palm against it from behind me.

"Please. Don't."

He's so close. A force of radiating heat that sticks to me and pulls. I keep my eyes on his splayed fingers still on the door.

"Jake."

His lips are on my neck and the heat, with that familiar masculine smell and the chill running down my back and arms are suddenly too much. His arms snake around me and he presses my back against his chest, his mouth and nose buried in my hair.

"Please," he whispers. I wrap my hands around his, still gripping me, and he makes a guttural sound of relief. He unwraps himself from me so quickly it feels like a whiplash, then presses me against him with the same force. My fingers find his hair and our mouths are gasping as we steal each other's breaths. It's not romantic, sweet, or tender. It's desperate, the quenching of a need that unleashes simultaneously inside both of us.

He lifts me and I wrap my legs around his waist. He carries me into the main room, then lowers me onto the dining table, pushing my legs apart as he pulls off my shirt, then my sweatpants with my swimsuit and my Ugg boots. I hear them meet the floor with a thud. As certain as what's about to happen between us.

He fucks me on the table, then we move to the couch where I sit astride him and take charge. It's a battle of wills against each other, and against our own inner selves urging us away from another bad decision.

We eventually make it to the bed. The animal rage has faded and there's only the two of us left. Jake makes love to me and I let him. I kiss him with abandon and with all the turmoil that stirs inside me.

Afterwards, I watch him sleep, the fear inside me pulsing under a cloud of fog. I know I can't give myself to this man, but I also can't deny the inevitability of what his presence does to me. He came back. He said he can't stay away. Could things have changed for him?

On the nightstand, the light of his cell phone goes on. He doesn't stir. I watch the lit screen from my side. It stays on for several seconds, taunting me. A text at two a.m. Morbid curiosity digs its claws into me, and before I know it, I slip out of the bed and walk around to his side. The text is still on his lit screen. A blade pierces my chest and finds my heart as I read it.

'I can't wait till next weekend, babe. Don't forget your swim suit. X. Rachel.'

Chapter 24: *Jake*

I turn on my side and she's gone. That sense of emptiness that fills me every time we say goodbye returns. I stare at the ceiling. The lack of control over my life ever since I met Natalia is starting to feel permanent. I can't allow that to happen, but I also need to acknowledge that the pull I feel for her is not going to give.

I have to find a way to make things with her work without losing a hold on my own feelings.

'*You can't love someone without giving them your whole heart, Jake.*' My father's words barge into my mind. *How did that work for you, Dad?*

No. My heart is not up for negotiation.

There's got to be a way to find balance without promises of happiness for all eternity. Promises end in disappointment when love finally ends. Why can't relationships be simple? Why can't people focus on the present without building a whole future in the air?

But I've seen the hurt in Natalia's eyes, and I know I can't keep doing this to her. There's got to be a way to make this work without anyone getting hurt. *There is. Walk away, Jake. Let her have a normal life with someone who gives a shit.*

The thought swells in my chest. No. I've tried running and it's led me right back here.

Maybe she'll be okay with a simple relationship where we both keep our independence. *Relationship?* My heart kicks at the word, but I stay on my train of thought. Natalia is about to start a new life in San Diego. A new job that will absorb most of her time and energy. The last thing she needs is a sappy boyfriend who demands attention. The more I think about it, the more sense my selfish plan makes in my head.

Maybe this can work.

I kick off the covers and head to the shower, eager to find her and see what she thinks of my proposition of living in the present with no strings attached. *You're a prince, Jake.*

I scurry through the employee hallway keeping my head down. When I reach her door, I knock softly and wait. The door swings open and there is Dani. Her head tilts to the side as she looks me up and down. Her eyes narrow. I think she's not happy with me.

"She's not here," she says.

"Oh. Where…"

"She went skiing."

"Do you know when she'll be back?"

She watches me for a long moment, probably questioning whether or not I deserve to know the answer.

"Anytime now," she mutters.

I turn to leave, but she grabs my arm. "Jake."

I stop in my tracks and turn to meet her eyes. They are like blue ice, deep and penetrating.

"Look," she says. "I don't know what's going down between you two. But you know as well as I do that Natalia just got her heart broken by that piece of shit fiancé of hers. The last thing she needs is a blow to the heart to finish her off."

"I wouldn't…"

"Natalia doesn't open up to people easily. Marc was the only guy she dated for most of the time I've known her. She's had a difficult life, and has worked her ass off to save for this internship and make her dream of being a chef a reality. Do not fuck this up for her, you hear me?"

She has articulated the perfect warning. All the things I have been pushing to the background, so they wouldn't conflict with my determination to make things work my way. Her eyes are locked on mine, waiting for my answer. Any words that cross my mind seem inadequate, or a flat out lie, so I don't say anything and answer with a single nod.

She lets out a sharp breath. "Good. I'm glad we're on the same page. I'll tell her you stopped by." Then she shuts the door in my face.

I stand there for a few seconds, trying to process, then head back to my villa. I won't know what happens next until Natalia and I talk.

Another half hour goes by, and I'm ready to punch something. I need to get out of here. I'm grabbing my coat when there's a knock on the door. I let out a sigh of relief. When I open it, she's standing there, beautiful as always in a long overcoat that drowns her delicate frame. I smile and swing the door all the way open. The moment she steps in I pull her into my arms. She smells like she just took a shower. Flowers and sun. *Sappy, Jake.*

"You left so early," I mutter against her hair.

"Yeah."

I wait for her to say more, but she doesn't. She seems somber. This morning I assumed she'd left because she had to work, but the fact that she went skiing means she left because she wanted to. I rack my brain for something that might have upset her, but come up empty.

"Are you okay?" I pull away to look into her eyes. They seem endless.

"I don't know," she says. I take her hand and lead her to the couch. I need to fix this, one way or the other. I know it's hurting her.

"Why did you come back, Jake?" Her voice is low, hesitant.

"I told you. I needed to see you."

"Okay, you've seen me. Now what?"

"What do you want, Natalia?"

She looks at me for a long moment, as if she's searching for the right words.

"I don't know," she says, finally. "But it's not this. This...hurts."

Her sincerity disarms me. I'm used to concealing my own feelings, even from myself. She's not like that. "Why did you leave this morning?"

She shrugs. "A text came in while you were sleeping. I saw it."

Fuck. Rachel's text. I should have turned my phone off. But she knows what I do for a living. Why is this a problem now?

"Babe," I say, searching her eyes. "You know enough of me to know I can't make promises for the future. I'm not wired like that.

Besides, relationships make people vulnerable." *Wow, Jake. You've just reached a new level, you selfish prick. Let the girl go.*

"I'm pretty fucking vulnerable right now, Jake. And this is not even a relationship."

"I don't want to hurt you."

"I know," she says, looking down. "Look. Maybe we end this here. I have a lot to do when I move to San Diego. I've worked hard to get there. I don't want to ruin that because I'm stuck in some fling with no future."

I shrug. "I wouldn't call this a fling. But maybe a relationship with no future is exactly what you need right now. Something that won't take anything away from your dreams and what you want." As I say this, I realize the extent of my assholeness. *Let her go.*

Her eyes are still focused on her hands. "I don't know Jake. There are some things I don't think I can deal with."

"Like?"

"Like your lifestyle. I don't want to be with someone I know is with other women. That bothers me, and since that's actually your *job*, well, maybe that says it all."

I run my hands through my hair. There's no dodging it now that she's articulated it. *Fuck.* My job is not up for negotiation. During the last few weeks, I've been toying with the idea of retirement, but if and when that happens I want it to be my decision. It can't be for anyone else. But we're standing at a crossroad, and I need to find a way out of this, or it will in fact end here.

"Natalia. I'm not trying to change who you are."

"I know, Jake. It's not really fair of me to ask you to do that either. You told me what you do from the beginning. I didn't expect to feel anything for you. But now…"

I lean toward her and press my forehead to hers. "I don't want to say goodbye."

Chapter 25: *Natalia*

We're standing at the edge of the cliff. If Jake lets go, I will fall. Maybe he's right, and the kind of relationship he's offering is what I need right now. Making careful plans with someone didn't work out the way it was supposed to.

So I make my decision.

"Okay, Jake. Maybe we can try and see if this works. We live in the present. We don't ask for more. I have just one request."

He tilts my chin up and presses a soft kiss on my lips. "What's that?"

"We always tell each other the truth."

Relief crosses the warm background of his eyes. "Deal." He takes my face in his hands and crushes me into a kiss. I'm grateful to be distracted from what I have just agreed to. A deal that may very well result in the biggest heartbreak I have ever experienced. I shift around so I'm straddling him and wrap my arms and legs around him without breaking the kiss. His arms move to my back and press me so tight against him there is no physical separation between our bodies. I get lost in the feeling of being in Jake's arms, knowing I have given up the more and settled for the less.

In the next two days, I'm not able to change my shifts, but spend every second I'm not working, with Jake. A huge weight has lifted now that we've defined the boundaries. The simple fact that I know when we will see each other again calms my anxiety. I just have to train myself to not wonder where he goes when he's not with me.

The new surf shop in San Diego will take most of his time for the next few months and that comforts me because it probably means he won't have a lot of time left for his *other* job. Maybe if I keep him busy enough…

The more I think about it, the more our arrangement seems manageable. Who knows where things will go. For the first time in my life I'm in a relationship where I don't know the outcome and I think that may be a good thing. I thought I had a sure hold on my relationship with Marc, but it took me to a dead end. At least with Jake there will be no lies. I can live with the rest.

I think.

Jake says he can stay for just one more day because he needs to start moving things into his San Diego apartment. I'm excited about the thought of both of us living in the same city. He will move in about a week and I have two more weeks left in Aspen. I have already signed the lease for a small condo in Coronado, and the excitement to begin my new life makes the hours go by slowly.

On Jake's last day we go skiing, then we have dinner at his villa. We are sitting on opposite ends of the couch, our bare feet touching. I've not felt this relaxed in a very long time. I'm in a blissful cloud of post-coital happiness with this godly man whose only flaws are to exist exclusively in the present and to keep his heart in a sealed armor.

Jake is trying to find a movie while I throw popcorn kernels at his mouth, trying to score. He scrolls down the options on the TV screen, whipping his head around and opening his mouth when I prompt him. My aim is awful, but Jake has lightning reflexes and makes it every time. He must have been one hell of a goalie.

"I wish I could have seen you play water polo." I smile and his eyes meet mine. "You must've been quite a show to watch."

His answering grin is disarming. I slide the bowl of popcorn to the floor and crawl onto his lap.

"Do you miss it?" I press a soft kiss on his lips. They taste salty from the popcorn, so I kiss them again and he smiles. "Tell me."

"Yes, I miss it. When you feel so much passion for something, it never leaves you." His eyes are intense and bright, then they quickly dart to the TV. "Pete has me teach clinics at his club from time to time, and it all comes back."

"Why aren't you a coach?"

He shrugs without taking his eyes off the TV. "The money sucks."

I look at his profile for a long moment. When he turns to meet my eyes, I close them and kiss him again. I don't want him to see the emotions that I'm sure cross my expression as I am, once again, reminded that Jake's choices steer him away from deep feelings, and lead to things he can control. Like money.

Sex is once again an effective distraction, and I spend the night in his arms, cherishing every minute we have together.

When Jake leaves the next morning, I don't dread it. I'm looking forward to what's ahead.

Dani, Zack and I wind up our last week at the lodge. Saying goodbye to everyone is harder this time because I know that, for me, it's the last time. Dani and Zack will visit me in San Diego this summer, and that makes saying goodbye to them a little easier.

This proves to be a year of curveballs and firsts. Instead of flying back to Buenos Aires right away, Dani is going to visit Dillon in San Francisco for a few weeks. She will take her final on the next calling in a few months. I look at her in shock and shake my head, but she has a face-splitting grin when she tells me and it's hard to not grin back. At first, I thought Dillon was a player, but something about the way he looks at her makes me believe that what he feels for her is real.

I hug them tight before I leave for the airport. Dani leaves tomorrow, and Zack the day after. I tell Zack for the millionth time to keep his promise to visit me. He smiles and tells me he will.

I check in at the airline counter and drop off my bags. My entire life is stuffed into two large suitcases and a duffel bag. Not much to sum up the last twenty-three years of my existence.

At the moment, Jake is somewhere between Santa Monica and San Diego, managing his own move. We made no plans except that I would call him when I was settled into my apartment. I have two days to get acquainted with my new environment before my internship begins on Monday. Excitement crawls on my skin like an army of ants.

I can't manage to sleep during the flight, so I open my iPad and start Leah Reader's new novel. She always manages to suck me out of the real world.

By the time we land, my nerves have left me exhausted. I wait for my bag at the carousel, looking at the fading afternoon sun through the airport windows. San Diego is bright, and everything here seems lighter and happier. I think it's the perpetual sun, and after more than three months under the Aspen snow, I'm looking forward to the change. It's only the beginning of the spring, but people walk around the airport in T-shirts, shorts, and flip flops.

I'm gonna like it here.

I see my bags and load them onto a cart. As I cross the sliding doors to the outside, I breathe in a lungful of warm salty air and smile. I roll my cart toward the curb to wait for the light, then a silver BMW pulls right beside me, blocking my way to the pedestrian crosswalk. I lean down to scowl at the driver, because that's flat out rude. But I freeze when I see Jake smiling from the driver's seat. My heart feels as if a bunch of fireworks just went off inside my chest. His smile widens as he slips out and rounds the car. He's wearing khaki board shorts and a white short-sleeve shirt. His roped arms are tanned underneath. The sight of him in summer clothes makes my breath catch. He looks like one of those lifeguards girls drool over in a TV series.

"I was hoping I'd catch you before you took a cab," he says, distracting me from my daydream. I'm still reeling from the shock of his presence.

"How did you…"

"I asked Dani for your flight information." He sweeps me up in a swift kiss, then lets go. I'm once again left wanting while he makes quick work of loading my suitcases into the trunk. I slip into the passenger seat still in a trance, trying to keep my emotions at bay.

I give Jake my apartment address and he pulls into the evening traffic. Coronado is an island connected to downtown by a massive bridge that curves over the San Diego Bay and a strip of sand on the other side. Jake merges onto the bridge onramp and I hold my breath. The view on both sides of it is spectacular. Little sailboats rock to and fro underneath, tiny strokes of paint on a deep blue canvas. The island is smaller than I imagined, but it's absolutely charming. Small houses are packed next to one another behind perfectly manicured yards. My condo is on Third Avenue, close to the landing where a ferry leaves every hour to downtown San Diego. Living here, I won't need a car right away. I can ride my bike to work and take the ferry if I want to leave the island.

Jake parks by the address I gave him and we both look up at my condo on the second floor. It's a small complex consisting of three apartments on the bottom and three on the top. I open my door and round the car, searching my bag for the key the landlady sent me a week ago. I'm supposed to meet her at her office tomorrow to sign the rest of the paperwork.

Jake gets my bags out of the trunk, then drops them and pulls me into a hug.

"Hi," he says against my lips. I kiss him and goose bumps travel down my arms. The familiar scent coming from him sends a swirl to my stomach.

"Thanks for coming, Jake." I smile and his answering grin is dazzling.

"You're welcome. I didn't want you to have to take a cab to your new place."

I nod, unable to stop smiling because, even though he makes no promises, this is a very nice welcome to my new city.

Inside, the apartment is simple, but well appointed. Everything is new including the carpet, and the walls are freshly painted. I look forward to adding things that will make it my own, but for now Jake is all I want to focus on.

We walk to a brewery on Orange Avenue, just two blocks away, and order fried calamari and beer. The evening is warm, and it's such a welcome change from the arctic cold of Aspen. Jake looks relaxed and tells me about the opening of his shop in a little over a week. He sounds excited as he describes what he has left to do in the next few days, wrapping up merchandise orders and finishing last minute preparations. I don't think I've ever seen him this enthusiastic, and it sends a warm feeling to my chest.

Back at my apartment door he asks me if I want him to let me rest. I answer him by clutching his shirt at the chest and tugging him inside with me. He smiles as he helps me pull it over his head.

I spend my first night in San Diego intertwined with Jake, his tanned arms and legs wrapped around my pale body like a vine. As I drift into an exhausted sleep, a spark of hope flicks my heart.

Chapter 26: *Jake*

As the next weeks pass, I have a good feeling this arrangement between Natalia and I is going to work. She looks happy, and so far she's given me no indication that she wants anything more. Her internship at the hotel leaves her little to no time off, and our schedules make seeing each other nearly impossible. When we finally get time together, we gladly take what the other one gives, and ask for no more. We are both exhausted. I'm already patting myself on the back because this is pretty close to perfect.

She switches her days off so she can help me with the opening of the shop. *Double Post* is set up to open in two days. The concept I created divides the store into two main sections: an area where we offer custom surfboards featuring a few floor models with cutting-edge designs, and a retail section dedicated to water polo gear including apparel, high end sunscreens, shampoos, and other cosmetics designed exclusively for swimmers and water polo players. It's the only surf shop of the sort, and I'm pretty excited with the prospect. I have met most of the retailers in the area, and everyone's been great about spreading the word. Cardiff is a small community of entrepreneurs and they welcome new concepts that are connected with the ocean and surf lifestyle in one way or another. Pete and Sydney have also been advertising my shop within their water polo club as the best place to purchase dedicated gear, so opening day is looking promising.

The day finally comes, and a crowd hovers at the door even before we open. Natalia helps me run through the last details and we are ready to go. Before we open the doors for the first time I wrap her in my arms.

"Thank you, babe. It means a lot that you are here," I tell her, because it's true. Her face lights up like a Christmas tree and she smiles.

Throughout the day, I walk around the floor and shake hands with people as they engage me in short conversations about the design of the store and the products and services we offer. There are quite a few customers from Pete and Sydney's club. They're eager to meet me and get their water polo playing kids' picture taken with an Olympic gold medalist. As a gift for the store opening, Syd had a few action shots blown up and framed from my days as a pro player. She turned one of them into wallpaper that panels an accent wall and I have to admit that she did an amazing job. I'm not thrilled at being the center of attention, but my reputation as a player proves to be a great marketing tool. I'm thankful to Pete and Syd for everything they've done to make this dream a success. *Shit*. I sound like an award winning speech.

Opening day is a smashing success. Pete, Syd, Natalia and I head to a local bar for a celebration dinner. Natalia and Sydney hit it off the second they met. I'm glad Syd and Pete approve of Natalia, given that I spend the only time off I have with her. Syd can't help herself and offers to introduce Natalia to a few members of the club who often hire a private chef for their dinners. Natalia laughs and reminds her she's still only an intern.

By the time we leave the bar, it's past midnight. Syd and Pete have to go back to their babysitter, and Natalia has to be at work early. We round the corner to my car. The night is warm. Natalia smiles as the ocean breeze lashes her hair onto her face.

"Why did you let me drink so much, Jake?" She laughs at her own wobbly walk and it's infectious. I scoop her in my arms and kiss her, pressing her against my chest. Her mouth welcomes mine. It's still sweet from the mojitos and it makes me want to kiss her all night.

"Jake, I'm proud of you," she says against my lips. "You've done it. You made your dream happen."

"So have you."

She smiles. "Not *quite*. I'm only the chef's apprentice. I have a long road ahead of me."

"You're on your way. Look at all the praise you've received from the management in just one month. I have no doubt you will accomplish everything you set that beautiful mind to." I close my eyes and kiss her forehead.

"I hope so," she whispers. And for some reason it makes me think she's not only referring to her job. I curse myself for letting my goddamn mouth run, then distract her with another kiss. We drive back to her place, and I invite myself for a sleepover.

In the morning, she wakes me with a kiss. Her lips taste like coffee and she smells fresh from the shower. I wrap my arms around her back and bring her down to the bed with me.

"Good morning. Are you leaving me already?" I kiss her again and she relaxes in my arms.

"Jake. I can't be late for work. The chef is in a bad mood even when I get it right. I don't want to give him any reasons to use me as his doormat today."

"Maybe I should come with you and have a word with him." I frown in mock irritation. Her eyes widen.

"What? *No*. Jake. Just…please, babe. Let me go." She laughs when I don't loosen my grip and she can't move. When all her attempts to push me away fail, she pouts. She knows I can't resist when she does that. I kiss her deeply and she moans.

"You're evil. I have to go." She pushes off me, but can't stop smiling. She looks happy. I get up from the bed and kiss her once again before she leaves. We won't see each other for another week. I have a three day trip booked with Rachel, one of my clients in Boston. Natalia doesn't know the details and she doesn't ask me where I'm going, but I'm sure her mind doesn't miss a beat. I haven't seen any of my clients since I moved to San Diego, and I don't want Natalia getting any ideas that our relationship is turning serious. We've finally reached a point of balance and I don't want to screw it up with unrealistic expectations and sappy boyfriend shit. *Charming, Jake.*

I meet Rachel on Tuesday at the Marriott in Copley Place in Boston. She has a couple of dinners planned and a charity event at a museum. Like Tamara, Rachel takes careful care of herself, and even though she's north of forty, she hardly looks over thirty-five. Rachel's favorite sport is hunting for rich husbands and she says I'm a 'delightful in-between.' Her red hair cascades down her back and she flicks it back with a perfectly manicured hand. I can't help thinking how she's the opposite of Natalia in every way. Nothing Rachel does is spontaneous. Every single move she makes is a step closer to what she wants. I have also never seen Rachel without makeup, never smelled and kissed her after a workout while she tells me I'm disgusting, the way Natalia did in Aspen. *Shit*. Rachel's a job and I don't know why in the fuck I'm thinking about Natalia when I'm supposed to be fucking working.

The minutes drag and I resent the fact that instead of enjoying this trip I'm dreading it. My mind drifts to the shop, and it's tough to stay connected with what used to be my full-time occupation. At the dinners, people talk about things I could care less about and I wonder how I ever found any of this remotely entertaining. The conversations are shallow and dull.

I make it through the first two dinners, and by the time the third event comes, I'm ready to walk away from Rachel the same way I did with Tamara. Come to think of it, I haven't talked to Tamara since. I wonder if she's already made Ryan my replacement. This would normally bother me, but at the moment all that occupies my mind is how I can get out of this trip with Rachel and go back home. *To her. You're slipping, Jake.* The realization that my thoughts are not only on the shop, but on Natalia, is sobering. I can't let that happen.

I don't want to end up like my father.

An image of him broken and lost after my mother left infiltrates my thoughts and the uneasiness in my chest churns like a giant meteorite.

Fuck, Jake. Keep this up and Natalia will walk away, too.

I push the uneasiness back to the dark place where it rose from, and resolve to follow through with my work commitments. My conscience can fuck off.

But as the weekend progresses, the sense of dread I feel expands. Even sex with Rachel leaves me empty, and for the first time since I started working as an escort, I feel like a whore. Every guy I know would give up his left nut to fuck Rachel. So what the hell do I have to complain about. *Maybe it's time for retirement.*

Rachel wants to book our next trip together, and I tell her I will call her during the week. None of my clients know about my shop, or any other detail of my personal life, so I keep my explanations vague.

As I fly home in first class, I'm convinced that at the very least I need to take a break. After what happened with Tamara, and almost again with Rachel, I should step away from my activities as an escort, or I will burn a lot of bridges. Deep down, I know a break is not a smart option if I decide I don't want to retire. My clients will find my replacement and I'm not willing to start over.

I run through the many possibilities in my head, over and over, and by the time I land, I've made my decision to retire. The store had an incredible start and even though I know sales will wind down after the novelty fades, I'm in no need of additional income.

When I land, I ask Pete to meet me for a quick drink so I can share the news. He congratulates me.

"About time. You're too old, Jake," he says, laughing it off. He's not all wrong. Even though I'm barely over thirty, the demand for a young ass is peaking among the forty year old clientele I cater to.

I resolve not to tell Natalia yet. I don't want her to think I'm ready to jump into another kind of relationship. I don't want to be with other women, but I need to hold on to my independence. I tell Pete to keep his mouth shut and not tell Sydney, since she and Natalia are quickly becoming good friends. He tells me I'm an asshole for keeping this from her, but agrees not to tell Syd, although he says it would make Syd happy to know I've left that lifestyle. Like Natalia, she's always hoped I would choose to do something else with my life.

The next few days, I see Natalia almost every night. I let my clients know about my decision to retire, and put them in touch with Ryan. Tamara and I have a long conversation. She was my first client, and in great measure is responsible for my successful career as an escort. She's been a great source of connections, and even though things never got personal between us, I feel a deep sense of appreciation for her. *Careful, Jake. That's almost a feeling.*

A few texts from my other clients come through during the week, some when Natalia and I are together. She knows I get messages from other women and doesn't say anything, but every time I can see a clear change in her expression. Sometimes she simply gets up and leaves the room. Afterwards we either get into an argument over something stupid, or one of us makes up an excuse and goes home. I'm glad I haven't told her about my retirement. She's getting a bit possessive, and I know where that will lead.

Thursday, I pick her up from work. I'm waiting outside on a bench and she eventually walks out, talking to a guy in a chef's coat. He looks like he's in his early thirties and smiles widely at her as she places a hand on his arm. He's listening to whatever she's telling him, standing a bit too fucking close for a coworker. She kisses his cheek and I close my hand into a fist as ire runs down my spine. Natalia turns in my direction and waves at me. I nod back and stand up, keeping my eyes trained on that fucker as he gingerly walks away.

"I didn't know you'd be here." She stands on her toes and kisses me.

"Clearly," I mutter.

She frowns. "What do you mean?"

I nod in the direction of the guy. "Making lots of new friends at work?"

She lets out an amused chuckle. "Excuse me?"

"Who was that?"

"Who was who?"

I raise an eyebrow. She does the same.

"Really, Jake?"

I press my mouth in a grim line. She has a point. I can't stake a claim without promising anything in return. For the first time, our agreement bites me in the ass. I run a hand through my hair to shake off my ridiculous sense of territory. I realize this is probably how she feels whenever my phone rings and it's a client. I have no right to feel this way, but the familiarity of her interaction with that prick still leaves a bitter taste in my mouth.

"Do we have plans?" she asks, and I'm glad for the change of subject.

"Yeah. Pete and Syd's house for dinner."

"Really?" Her face lights up and I can't help the smile it brings to mine. "Syd didn't say anything to me last night."

I shrug. "I think it was last minute."

I don't say much as I drive us back to her apartment. I wait for her to shower and dress, looking through the window at the approaching storm tinting the sky gray. The only image occupying my mind is her reaching up and kissing that fucker goodbye.

Chapter 27: *Natalia*

I help Sydney with the last dinner preparations while the guys get the barbecue ready and have drinks outside. Jake has been brooding ever since he picked me up from work. I tell Sydney about the way he reacted to me walking out with Charlie.

"Natalia, if I were you, I wouldn't even acknowledge it. He has no right to throw a fit."

"I know." I look down at the veggies I'm chopping. "I have to put up with all those women calling him. I wish he knew how much that hurts. I can't even think about it, even after all this time."

"Have you told him that?"

"No, Syd. I have no leg to stand on. Jake has never lied to me. He's always been straightforward about what he does. Besides if I bring it up, he'll run."

"Natalia. If you want a future with Jake, you both have to overcome this hurdle. You need to tell him how you feel and he needs to fucking get over his perpetual fear of commitment."

"I just wish I understood why a normal relationship freaks him out so much."

"Look, I've known Jake for a long time. He's always been that way. But it's no excuse." She pours me a glass of wine and switches to a lighter conversation about the latest happenings at the club. I'm relieved with the change of subject, and finish my wine. She refills my glass, then picks up her baby from her bouncy seat and slips her into the highchair to feed her.

"May I?" I ask, gesturing to the bowl and spoon she's holding. Syd smiles and hands them to me.

I feed baby Mia while she smiles and tries to grab the spoon. Syd scoops chopped mango on the tray of her chair and Mia squishes it as she brings it to her mouth with a grin. She doesn't want any more of the vegetables I'm feeding her, but when I pretend the spoon is an airplane, she's engaged again and finishes the whole thing.

"You're a pro, Natalia," Sydney says. "You're invited for dinner every night until Mia turns eighteen."

Jake walks in and his eyes lock on me as I'm wiping Mia's face and kissing her little hands. His expression stills for a moment and when our eyes meet his are guarded. Whatever his problem is tonight, I don't want any part of it. I'm tired from the long weekend at work while Jake was away who knows where with who knows who. I shake off the bitter thought and, ignoring Jake, get up to finish setting the table.

Dinner with Syd and Pete rolls into the late hours. Jake and I really enjoy spending time with them, and it often diffuses the tension between us. They are also my only friends in San Diego, aside from the few people I met at work. I like that Sydney knows Jake well, and that there is a lot about him I don't have to explain to her.

Jake and Pete walk to the car as they finish their conversation. Syd hugs me at the door, lingering a bit longer than usual.

"Be patient with him. He'll come around. He's just as stubborn as a goat. But I know you're special to him, Natalia."

I hug her again in response. When I look at Jake over her shoulder, he's watching us intently with that same guarded expression from before. What the hell is his problem?

The ride in the car is quiet. I'm beat. I have the day off tomorrow and am looking forward to sleeping in.

"What was going on between you and Sydney?" Jake says as he pulls into traffic.

"Nothing. Why?"

"When she hugged you goodbye you looked...I don't know. Upset."

I shake my head. "I'm not upset, Jake." I'm too tired to get into an argument, and honestly, even more tired to put up with whatever his reasons are to be so moody. I wish I had my own car. Jake lives in Cardiff near Syd and Pete, but has to drive across town to take me home. On nights like this one, I don't want any favors from him.

"I'm going to rent a car," I mutter.

Jake frowns. "Why?"

"I don't want to depend on you for every place I have to go to. It's not fair."

"I don't mind."

"Still. It'll give me more independence. Especially on the days when you're away."

He stays quiet for a long pause, his eyes lost on the road.

"I won't be traveling for a while. You don't need to rent a car."

This gets my attention. Is he cutting his hours at his *other* job? Even after all this time, I still can't call it what it is. *An* escort,

Natalia. Fancy word for whore. I'm dying to ask him what's changed. He's been in a bad mood since he came back.

"Jake, is everything okay?"

"Yes," he answers almost immediately. "Why wouldn't it be?"

I shrug. "You're in a strange mood tonight."

He eyes me speculatively and runs a hand through his hair.

"I've just got a lot of shit in my mind, is all." He doesn't explain further, and I know better than to ask. These conversations between us always end in an argument about unreasonable expectations.

He drops me off at home and kisses me briefly at the door. I don't invite him to stay over and he doesn't ask. I think we both need space tonight.

The next two days I'm off, but Jake is teaching a water polo clinic at Pete's club, so I don't see him. I spend my time visiting kitchen emporiums with two girls from work. We stock up on utensils and other tools we often use in the kitchen. I spend a large amount of my salary, but I'm happy with my new purchases. These are all things that will last me for years.

Pierre, the executive chef, selects me from within the interns to assist him in plating entrees. This is great because I get to stay in the kitchen as an apprentice and it temporarily excuses me from the next rotations on my schedule. I work my ass off so he keeps me here, and nowhere near the pool.

Chef Pierre has been great to me and has become my mentor. He loves learning about Argentina and my training at the culinary academy. As the week comes to an end, my prayers get answered and he asks me what rotations I have left at the hotel. I tell him I have completed everything except the pool and, when I confess to him that I'm afraid of swimming, he tells the management he needs me in the kitchen. Next thing I know I'm exempt. I almost hug him.

As the days progress, Chef Pierre adds more tasks to my schedule. I accept them gladly, eager to learn as much as I can. My ultimate dream is to work with Chef Pierre on his pastries. He's the best in the city and the main reason why I wanted to do the internship at this hotel. The rest of the interns seem a bit put-off by the favoritism. But in my defense, I never complain about the long hours or the monotonous work he throws my way.

I stay after hours so Chef Pierre can train me in-between shifts. There isn't much time for mistakes during the rush hours, so I use every minute he gives me. All my energy is focused on work. I don't see much of Jake that week except for dinner on Sunday night. We're both tired and he spends the night at my apartment, so we can at least fall asleep together.

The weeks that follow are busy. Jake is working full time at Double Post, and I'm finally getting bits of pastry training from Chef Pierre.

The hotel will soon offer one of the interns a permanent position on the staff. I have a good chance, I think, but so does Charlie. He and I have become good friends. If someone can take this dream from me, it's Charlie. He comes from San Francisco and his training at the culinary academy has prepared him well.

Charlie and I are in constant competition. We challenge each other, and I work harder than ever just to see the look of respect he gives me when I do something that impresses him. To me, Charlie's opinion matters as much as Pierre's.

Jake doesn't like Charlie. He hasn't come out and said it, because that would mean Jake has to own up to an actual feeling, but he's always in a bad mood if I walk out of work with Charlie. On those nights, he stays quiet, and most likely spends the night as his place in sulky protest.

As the weeks fly by, Jake is getting the hang of managing the shop and I start getting more normal hours. The girls I met at the internship constantly ask me to go out with them, but I'm always with Jake. At work, people tease me about my imaginary boyfriend. Only Charlie has seen Jake a few times, and he vouches for my sanity. I have told Charlie vaguely about my relationship with Jake. It's hard not to talk about personal stuff when we spend so much time together at work. Charlie and I usually take our breaks together and spend a long time talking. He had a girlfriend, but they broke up because she said he didn't have enough time off.

"It's better this way," Charlie says, taking a bite of his sandwich. We're taking our lunch break on a bench outside with a breathtaking view of the ocean.

"Did you love her?"

"I don't know." Charlie shrugs. "What about you, Nat? You *in love*?" he teases me.

I nod. "I think so, but if I told him he would freak out."

"You *haven't* told him?"

"No. I don't know. After Marc, I didn't want to make any plans with anyone. I just wasn't ready."

"Then don't make plans with anyone. But don't settle."

I look up at him. Charlie doesn't beat around the bush. You always know exactly where he stands. Maybe that's why he's so good at his job. He never hesitates when it comes to making a decision.

"Do you think I'm a linguini-spine, door-mat, or whatever else you guys call people that cannot put their foot down?"

Charlie laughs. "No. But once you figure out what you want, don't wait around for this guy to bring it to you. The way I see it, you either go for it, or are better off alone."

"Jesus, Charlie. Way to put the bullet between the eyes."

He winks at me, then scrunches up his trash and stands up. "Let's go."

Charlie's words simmer in the back of my mind all day. The following night, I invite Jake for dinner at my place after he closes Double Post. Jake loves it when I cook for him, which I don't get to do a lot due to our miss-matched schedules. For tonight, I rolled homemade pasta and sautéed scallops in a white wine sauce. I'm finishing the *Alfajores* I made for dessert, when Jake walks in.

"Whatever that is, it smells amazing." He smiles and saunters toward me, then hugs me from behind and kisses my neck. I'm rolling the *Dulce de Leche* filled cookie sandwiches onto shredded coconut and both my hands are busy. His lips tickle my neck and I shiver.

"What are those?" he says over my shoulder. I love Jake's enthusiasm when it comes to food. He's always appreciative of whatever I make for him, and acts as if it's the most amazing thing he's ever tasted. I explain that the cookies are an Argentinean staple, and describe how I made them. He wants to try one, and when I feed it to him, he closes his eyes.

"Hmmm," he moans in appreciation, then pulls me into his arms and kisses me. I can taste the sweetness in his mouth. "I'm the luckiest bastard on earth."

I smile, because he always says that.

We eat dinner on the floor, propped up against the couch. Jake says he loves everything, and we take turns feeding each other bites. When we are done, he refills our wine glasses and sits the plate with pastries between us. He closes his eyes every time he eats one, and it makes me smile.

"You have to make me these for my birthday, babe. I don't even want a cake. I just want a box full of these."

"I love that you like my food, Jake." I grin.

"I never had a woman cook for me before." He pops another cookie in his mouth. I frown.

"Seriously?"

"Seriously." He nods and takes a sip of wine. He looks uncomfortable.

"Your mom didn't cook?"

He stills, then takes another sip of wine. I've never asked Jake about his mom, and whenever he talks about his family he never mentions her. "No," he mutters, then puts his glass down and pulls me onto his lap to kiss me. "Thank you, babe. This was amazing."

"You're welcome." I look into his eyes and want to tell him the words that want to burst out of me whenever we are like this.

I'm falling for you, Jake.

Jake pulls me into a kiss, distracting me. I give in, but Charlie's words come back to me, and I know that he's right. After Marc and I broke up, it was all an avalanche. I need to think of what I want. Maybe what I need is to be alone for a while and figure things out.

And as Jake kisses me, a new ticking sound pulses inside me.

***

Dani and Zack finally come to visit me. I'm thrilled to see them. Dillon will come down from San Francisco for the weekend, too.

Chef Pierre gives me an extra day off when I tell him I have friends visiting from Buenos Aires. It's unusual, but he knows how hard I work and I promise to make it up the following week.

My internship ends in a month and so does my visa. If I'm not offered a job at that time, I will have to go back to Buenos Aires. This causes my anxiety level to fly off the charts. Sydney tells me to apply to all the restaurants in town as a backup, and assures me I will find a job easily.

I'm not so sure.

Dani and Zack are stretched out opposite each other on the only couch in my living room, while I make cocktails and tell them about having to find a job soon.

"You could marry Jake," Dani says, yawning at the ceiling.

I drop the ice in the glasses and peek around the door.

"Dani. That's *illegal*."

"So? Lots of people do it."

I laugh. "Can you imagine? Jake would have a stroke."

"If after all this time he still can't man-up he can fuck off, Nati," Zack says from his end of the couch. Dani nods. She knows about Jake's other job, but Zack doesn't. If he did, I know for a fact he'd find Jake and beat the shit out of him. Zack may not be six four, but he can win a fist fight against pretty much anyone. I have actually witnessed it a few times. He's absolutely fearless.

So what are you going to do?" Dani asks.

"Seriously guys, can you quit dumping on me? You just got here."

Zack rubs his forehead. "I just don't get why you insist on dating American guys. They all have fucked up morals, or commitment shit."

I carry their drinks to them and Zack smiles. He loves it when the tables are turned and I make drinks for him.

"Dani, how are things with Dillon?"

She grins. "*Amazing*. I'm madly in love." She laughs and Zack and I look at each other. "I know...I sound like one of those high school brats. But seriously. I never thought I'd fall this hard for a guy. He's come to Buenos Aires twice since we left Aspen. I'm worried he'll be broke soon."

I sit on the floor with my back against the couch and my legs stretched in front of me. I take a sip of my mojito, wishing Jake was a little bit like Dillon.

"Let's go out tonight," Zack says.

I look up at him. *Yeah*. Let's go out tonight.

Chapter 28: *Jake*

There's a knock on the door as I get out of the shower. I throw on jeans and swing it open. Dillon grins as he looks me up and down.

"Man, I hope I interrupted something good."

I roll my eyes. "Nice to see you, asshole."

He drops his bag by the door and goes straight to the fridge to grab a beer, then tosses me one. He wasn't supposed to show up till tomorrow, but he said he wanted to surprise Dani.

"So tell me about this girl. You've flown to Buenos Aires twice already. Is she the real thing?"

He takes a swig of his beer and sucks his lips in. "Yup. Think so."

I watch him while I drink mine. This whole thing with Dani is so out of character for Dillon. I've never seen him like this about a woman.

"You're starting to freak me out, Dillon." I laugh. "Are you going to marry her and shit?"

A corner of his mouth curves up. "Possibly. Who knows. I have a surprise for her tonight."

My chest tightens and I take a long swig of beer. "Shit, man. Don't tell me you're proposing 'cause I'll have to beat some sense into you."

Dillon laughs. "Nope. Not that. Not yet, at least."

Immediate relief washes over me. I grill Dillon further, but whatever his surprise is, he's tight lipped. I agree to come with him to Natalia's where Dani is staying.

We knock on Natalia's door after nine, but the place is silent. I text her and she tells me they're at a bar downtown. Dillon and I finally make our way there. It's a bitch to find parking, and I have to be up early to do inventory. I'm glad he drove his rental, so I give him a key to my place and tell him I'll probably leave the bar early.

We find the girls at a table with their other friend, Zack. He gives me a guarded look as I shake his hand. I don't think he likes me. Dani jumps at the sight of Dillon. He scoops her in his arms and gives her a deep kiss in front of everyone. We all whistle at their explicit show.

I buy the next round of drinks, and Natalia tells me she's already on her third, but it's okay because she doesn't have to work tomorrow. She looks tipsy, but for the first time in a while, she also seems relaxed.

We order food and keep the drinks coming. Dani is on Dillon's lap and they have not spent a single moment apart. Poor asshole, he's whipped. The waitress is clearing the food off our table when Dillon stands up. I'm thinking he's heading to the bathroom, but he pulls on Dani's hand and tugs her away toward a patio at the back of the restaurant. I follow them with my eyes and see Dillon wrapping her into his arms as he says something to her ear. Whatever he says to her makes her squeal out loud and she jumps back into his arms and kisses him. What the fuck. I hope he didn't just propose. That would make me an even bigger asshole in front of Natalia. *Nice, Jake. Always the selfish fuck, aren't you.*

They come back to the table and tell us they have an announcement. My palms are fucking sweating because this sounds a hell of a lot like a proposal. I want to punch Dillon for not giving me a heads up. But then he announces he will spend the next year in Argentina with Dani. He will look for a job, and then they'll see where things go from there. Dani can't stop crying. You'd think she just won the lottery. *Maybe Dillon* is *her lottery.* Huh. My eyes lock with Dillon's as he slides into the seat across from me. I shake my head and he smirks.

"Sorry. I needed to tell her first."

I dismiss him with a nod. Dillon is fucking crazier than I thought. "Good luck, man," I mutter. I turn to Natalia and she's looking at Dani with something like longing. Her eyes are wet and I can tell she's trying not to cry. I hold her hand under the table.

"Want to dance?"

She doesn't look at me, but nods and slides out of the booth. I wrap her in my arms, and when I look down at her, she quickly wipes her eyes. I feel like the biggest shit in the world because I know I'm somehow responsible for those tears. I brush her hair to the side so I can kiss her neck. She melts, the way she always does when we are this close and I take a deep breath of my favorite smell.

"Are you okay?" I whisper.

She nods, then closes her eyes and the tears spill again. I wipe them with my thumbs. "Please don't. I hate to see you sad, Nati."

For some reason this makes her cry harder. She presses her face against my chest to hide her eyes and I tighten my arms around her.

"Do you want to go?" I ask her, and she says yes.

I give her a few minutes to dry her eyes, then she says goodbye to Dani and gives a key to Zack in case she's asleep when he comes back to her place.

In the car she's quiet. I rack my brain for something to lift her mood, but I'm at a loss. When we reach her apartment door I kiss her.

"Do you want me to stay?"

She looks at me for a long moment. "This doesn't work for me anymore, Jake."

A claw of panic grips my chest.

"What?"

"Our arrangement. I thought I could do this, but I can't." She turns to unlock the door.

"What are you saying?" My heart is kicking the shit out of my ribcage. I pull her into the apartment and turn on the lights, then pace around. The walls close in on me. *Fuck*. This can't be happening. "Natalia. Everything was fine until tonight. What the hell happened?"

"I'm in love with you, Jake. I have been for a while, and I can't hold all this in anymore. It's killing me."

I run both hands through my hair as the panic rises to my throat. This feels like a fucking nightmare, the moment I've been dreading since I decided to give this a shot.

"Natalia. What the fuck. We had an agreement."

"Why?" she snaps. "What the hell happened to you that you've chosen to live your entire life without mustering a single feeling?"

"I've never lied to you. I told you from the start I don't get involved in relationships that way. You knew this about me. You said you were okay with it." Now it's me who's shouting. I have to close my hands into fists to stop the shaking. Her eyes narrow.

"How can I be okay knowing every time you leave you fuck other women for money? What the hell does that say about me? I must be more screwed up than you. I'm sorry, Jake. I just can't keep this going."

"The women," I mutter. "They're over. I don't do that anymore. I'm retired."

She walks around me and searches my eyes. "What did you say?"

"I'm retired." I look down at her and her eyes are drawn in confusion.

"Since when?"

I close my eyes for a moment. I know exactly where this is going, but I have promised not to lie to her, and I need to keep that promise.

"A few months ago."

Her eyes lock on mine in an incredulous stare as her mouth falls open.

"A few *months*? Why didn't you tell me, Jake?"

"I didn't want you to think I was ready for something different between us."

"Oh my God. Do you have any idea how fucked up that is?"

The tears filling her eyes spill as she blinks.

"I'm sorry, Natalia."

"You are? *Sorry?* You selfish son of a bitch. What the hell is wrong with you? Do you know what it's been like to wake up every morning knowing you may be fucking someone else later on?"

"Natalia—"

"It fucking *killed* me. Every. Fucking. Day. You're so incredibly selfish that you kept it from me because God forbid the great Jake Harper articulates a goddamn feeling for once." Her fist is pounding on my chest, but I don't defend myself. I let her run out of air. Then she lets her arms drop. She's sobbing so hard her whole body is shaking. I wrap my arms around her and hug her for a long time. She doesn't hug me back, but she has no energy left to fight me. I slide us to the floor and pull her onto my lap, closing my arms around her. She doesn't say anything. She just cries against my chest until her sobs are barely audible. I lean my cheek on her head and we stay like that for a long time. Then she pulls away and looks into my eyes.

"I want more, Jake." Her eyes are pure, crystal green. Panic unfurls inside me.

"I can't," I mutter. "I'm sorry, Natalia. I can't."

Her palms press against my chest and she pushes me away.

"Then go." Those blazing green eyes meet mine and narrow.

"You don't mean that."

"I do. I need you to go and let me live my own life. Do not come back, Jake. If you're half the man I thought you were, you'll respect my decision and stay away from me."

"This is what you want?" My heart is banging in my chest. I know if I leave here tonight I won't have another chance with her.

"Yes." Her expression is calm. She stands up and turns, then disappears into her bedroom. I expect her to slam the door, but she doesn't. I stand up in automated motion and close the front door behind me.

And as I make my way to my car, all hell breaks loose inside of me.

***

I drive around for hours, at a complete loss of what to do next. In my mind, parting ways with Natalia has always been a possibility. What I didn't factor in was *her* breaking up with *me*. *Of course, Jake. That would have meant your overinflated ego needed a checkup.*

I pull over by the landing, now deserted. Clutching the steering wheel, I press my forehead to my hands as what feels a hell of a lot like a panic attack explodes in my chest.

You're an idiot, Jake. Yes. I'm an idiot. And an egotistic fuck for thinking she would never leave me.

I walk to the shore and sit on the sand with my head in my hands. The furious roar of the ocean is deafening, and all at once the memories from my past flood my mind. I squeeze my eyes shut, but there is no stopping the tornado as it thrashes through my head. I fist my hair to stop the trembling in my hands. The darkness is unleashed, and it's so loud inside my head, my brain is pulsing. Two decades of unshed tears scald my eyes. I cry out loud as a tidal wave of pent-up emotions scourges its way through me. I can't hold back and break down in a convulsion of sobs.

And the day my mother left comes back like it was yesterday.

I'm eight. Our life at the ranch in Santa Barbara is simple, but we're happy, my brother Jamie, Mom, Dad, and me. Jamie has just turned four and we had a party for him.

In the evening Mom comes to my room and sits down on my bed. I tell her I can't wait to start swim camp the next day. She looks at me for a long time, then tells me she's leaving that night and won't live with us anymore. She says she has to leave because the love she once felt for my dad is gone. I don't understand. We are happy. I don't want to be like those kids at school with just one parent. I start crying and beg her not to go. She caresses my hair and lets me cry. She says she will always love Jamie and me, and that she's sorry she can't be a better mother. She says I have to be strong for Jamie and for Dad. Jagged pain churns inside my chest.

I don't go to swim camp. Every day, Jamie and I wait on the front steps of our house. Jamie keeps saying mom will come back for us, and although I know she isn't, I can't squash the little hope he has left. One day, it's really cold when we go out. We sit for a long time. Jamie is shivering hard, and I tell him we should go in. He won't listen so I grab his face and yell that mom is a selfish person and she isn't coming back. After that day, Jamie cries himself to sleep for I don't know how many nights. Until one day he wakes up and the light in his eyes is gone. He stops smiling.

As the memories come flooding back, so does the hatred. I have hated that woman every day since the day she left. I hated her for me and for Jamie and for Dad. Dad never lost hope. He forgave her, and so did Jamie.

Not me.

It took so long for the pain to ease.

Maybe it never did.

I have never openly talked about this to anyone. Not even Pete. But I need Natalia to know the truth. I need her to know that I would love her if I could.

I drive back to her apartment. The lights are off, but I can't leave until I do what I came here to do.

I knock on the door and within minutes it swings open. Her eyes are swollen and red rimmed. Her lip trembles and she shakes her head.

"Jake…"

Before she has time to say anything, I let the words out in a torrent. I don't even come in. I stand at her threshold afraid that if I take one step in, I won't be able to go through with this. I grip the door frame to stop the shaking. My breaths are coming out in broken gasps as I fight for control.

I tell her everything about that day. About my mother leaving, about Jamie and Dad. About the misery she left us in. I don't stop until she knows everything I've been withholding about my past.

"I saw how my father's life faded away every single day. I can still see the look in his eyes. The heartbreak. He always told me he never regretted loving her. He said some people are broken and can't cope with the pain. He said my mother loved us, but she was ill and not equipped to be a mother. I hated her. Every day. I promised myself I would never let a woman do that to me."

Natalia watches me with wide eyes and leans on the door, winded. Tears stream down her cheeks. She's trying to stifle her sobs, but her body is shuddering.

"I love you, Jake. I'm not her."

The words cut through me.

No.

I turn around and take the stairs two at a time.

Chapter 29: *Natalia*

I fall face down on my bed. Part of me knew this day was coming. That part has been preparing, storing up numbness for precisely this moment. The rest of me is raw with sheer pain. It's like I'm being burned alive. The day that plastic chick opened Marc's door was only a shred of what I feel right now. A full room of words wouldn't be enough to describe it.

So I don't even try.

I cry most of the night until I finally have no tears left. In the morning, I step around Zack who is sound asleep on the living room couch. I'm glad he's here. It will help me be strong if Jake decides to come back to persuade me, the way he always does. Although, this time, I know there's no coming back for me.

When Zack wakes up, we go out for breakfast. He knows something is up because I haven't taken my sunglasses off, even though the sun hasn't yet made an appearance.

"Shitty night?" he says, taking a bite of his waffles.

"More like shitty six months."

"That bad, huh? You and Aquaman having problems?"

I ignore his joke and push my food around with my fork. "We broke up."

"Fucker. Seriously? I knew that guy couldn't be trusted. He better not show his face at your place. What'd he do?"

"Nothing. That's just it. No future."

"Shit. Well, better now than later then, Nati."

"I need to get a grip, Zack." I mutter. "First Marc, then Jake. I can't let guys drive my life. I need to be the one at the wheel."

We finish our breakfast, and I feel like going back to bed, but I don't want to ruin Zack's short visit. Dani spent the night with Dillon. She comes by in the morning when she finds out what happened. She hugs me while I have a crying fit after I find one of Jake's T-shirts in my laundry basket. She says Jake was out of the apartment last night, and when he showed up in the morning, he looked like shit. The fact that Jake is miserable too should comfort me, but it doesn't.

Sydney calls me a few times to talk, but I tell her I need a few days. I can't talk about Jake.

Zack and Dani go shopping, and I spend the morning at the beach on my own. I think of all the things that have happened over the last few months. Where did it all go wrong?

That evening Zack and I go out for beers with some people from work. Charlie and Zack hit it off right away. It's good to be around people and it temporarily distracts me from my own thoughts. My work is the only place where there are no memories of Jake.

Outside of work, Jake is everywhere.

Chapter 30: *Jake*

The first rays of sun stretch from afar. The sky goes from black to indigo and the soothing sound of the waves wakes me. I get up, stiff from hours without moving, and head back to my apartment for a shower. Today will be a busy day at the shop and I'm vaguely relieved it will keep my mind busy.

But as the day advances, focusing on anything becomes fucking impossible. I do the inventory, but have to count the same things two and three times, and I'm pretty sure my employees think I'm a complete moron.

By the time I close the shop, all I want is to get drunk. I buy a bottle of *Glenlivet* at the liquor store and head back toward the beach. I don't want to be in my apartment in case Dillon and Dani are there. The beach does not allow alcohol, so I roam around in my car without a better plan. Before I know it, I'm crossing the Coronado bridge.

I park at the corner near her apartment, and kill the engine. The lights are off, so she must be out. Did she already move on? The thought of her at a bar laughing at some prick's jokes makes my blood boil. Maybe she's with that fucker she works with, Charlie. I can't stand the guy, always hovering around her. I take a swig and welcome the burn of the alcohol as it slides down my throat. I take another long swig, then another. I stop before it's too late and I'm too drunk to drive.

She comes home after one in the morning. I watch her get out of a cab with Zack and make a tipsy line to her apartment. At least she's with Zack. He's protective and probably kept all the assholes in the bar away from her.

I get out of the car without any idea of what I'm doing next. I just want to see her. Know she's okay.

No. That's not it.

I want to see that she's *not* okay. I know that if she sees me, I may have a chance to put this back together.

We can't be over. *Brilliant plan, asshole.*

Zack opens the door and asks me what the fuck I'm doing there. *Good question.* He looks pissed, and his eyes narrow when I don't respond right away. I tell him I need to see Natalia. He tells me to fuck off, and when I try to push past him he clutches my shirt, and before I can blink, his fist snaps against my jaw. I fall back a few steps, but manage to grip the handrail. I want to take him out, but he's protecting her from me, which is exactly what she needs right now.

A second later, she appears at the door wearing only a T-shirt. A fucking tornado thrashes my chest. The last time she wore that she was in my bed and I was wrapped around her. Her eyes are wide and red rimmed, her hair falling over her shoulders in an untamed mess. She looks beautiful. I can see the conflict in her expression and I want to tell her we can work this out. She belongs with me.

But Zack pulls her back into the apartment and slams the door before I can take a step and scoop her in my arms.

Chapter 31: *Natalia*

There's a knock on the door and Zack goes to it.

Jake.

Then the distinct sound of a fist against flesh. I bolt to the door and Jake is down a few steps, his body half bent forward as he holds his jaw. Blood is trickling down from the corner of his mouth.

"Get the fuck out," Zack growls, then grips my shirt and pulls me back inside with him as he slams the door.

"Don't cave, Nati. You deserve better than him." He pulls me into his arms. I nod against his chest because he's right.

I take a sleeping pill and don't wake up till the next morning when Zack shakes me.

"Your alarm's been going off for the last five minutes, Nati."

I rush through my morning routine and go to work while Zack and Dani go paddle boarding with Dillon.

I'm eager to lose myself in the fast-paced environment of the kitchen. Charlie doesn't ask me how I'm doing, and I'm relieved. I told him about my breakup with Jake last night and he seemed concerned about me. He's more attentive than normal and I tell him I need him to challenge me and stop babying me. Charlie smiles, and tells me he'll make me wish I had never said that.

The next morning Zack, Dani, and I, cross the Mexican border and drive an hour to Rosarito, a touristy little town on the beach. We spend my two days off having margaritas and street tacos. It's a welcome change of scenery with no memories from the past. It's good to be with my friends, and finally celebrate our graduation from cooking school. The atmosphere is light and Mexicans are friendly and unconcerned in general. The three of us leave everything behind and have a good time.

Zack leaves, and without him, the apartment feels empty. On the days that follow, Dani spends most of my time off with me and away from Dillon. I don't want her to worry about me, so I assure her I will be fine. The best thing for me right now is to focus on work and not dwell on what happened with Jake.

She and Dillon leave to San Francisco a few days after and even though I will miss her, I'm glad to be alone with nothing that connects me with Jake.

Syd and I talk on the phone a lot, and a few times she drags me out to dinner. I don't ask her about Jake, and she doesn't bring it up. Our conversations stay around the club and the latest gossip in the kitchen. It is only inches at a time, but I slowly feel like I'm moving forward.

The days turn into weeks with a slow, automated rhythm, and before I know it, a whole month has gone by since the last time I saw Jake at my door. Sometimes when I come home at night, I feel like he's somewhere close by. But it's always my imagination playing tricks. Jake is gone. The only noise in the air is the sycamores fluttering their leaves as they prepare for the fall.

I only have a month left in the internship. They will announce the winner of the permanent position on the staff in the next two weeks. Charlie and I are neck and neck, and even though Chef

Pierre favors me, the management loves Charlie. He's got that charisma that makes everyone instantly like him.

On the days before the announcement of the position, I push myself beyond my limits. I want this job badly. I also send my resumé to a couple dozen hotels in the area. Chef Pierre is being very tight lipped about the whole thing, but has agreed to give me letters of recommendation after I beg. If something can help get me a job, it's Chef Pierre's reputation.

On the day of the Chef's announcement, Charlie and I stand side by side next to the rest of the interns. He reaches for my hand and squeezes it. My heart is racing, and I feel like I'm about to pass out. There is no oxygen in this kitchen, and I don't know why Chef Pierre and the hotel manager are taking so goddamn long to put us out of our misery.

The general manager thanks us for our immeasurable dedication and all the hard work we have given to the hotel during our internship. All I hear is blah, blah, blah, position, and blah, blah permanent, and blah staff, and…Charlie Hunt.

Charlie.

Not me.

I turn around to hug him and he simultaneously does the same. Then he pulls away, and presses his forehead to mine.

"*Fuckdammit*," he mutters. I smile because Charlie never swears.

"You fucking earned it, Charlie," I tell him.

Charlie gets ambushed by the rest of the staff, and shakes hands with Chef Pierre and the management, who take turns congratulating him and welcoming him to the staff.

I'm disappointed, but it's hard to surrender to that feeling when I lost to Charlie. I'm genuinely happy for him, despite what this means for me. Chef Pierre gives me an embrace and tells me he's saddened to see me go. "I wanted it to be you," he says. And I believe him. He assures me he's made some calls on my behalf, and I thank him with a heavy heart. I hold the tears until I get home.

Then I let it all out.

The two reasons why I came to the U.S. have ended up in grand failures. Both Marc and a job working with Chef Pierre are now bleached-out dreams. For the first time since I left Aspen, I think of Marc and all the plans we once made together. Then I think of Jake, and the plans we never made. Which was worse?

No. I'm not going there.

I have to keep going forward. Having worked under Chef Pierre will open doors for me.

I can't let this be it.

I have two weeks left of the internship and start my interviews. The next day I have the first one at a hotel in Del Mar and have a few more lined up over the next three weeks.

The interview in Del Mar goes well, and I meet with the executive chef. He is a close friend of Chef Pierre's, and I hope that helps. If I don't find a job in the next three weeks, I will have to go back home to Buenos Aires. The thought depresses me. I have fallen in love with San Diego, and I want to find a job here.

Charlie and I walk out as the day ends. The staff is going out for drinks later, and he's making his case to get me to come. I'm about to agree, but then look up, and my heart jumps into my mouth. I skid to a halt.

Marc.

He's standing at the curb, leaning on his black Maserati. *Shit.*

Charlie's eyes are now locked on Marc, too. Or on his car, I'm not sure.

"You know him? Sweet ride."

"Yeah," I mutter. Marc smiles at me and shrugs. I look up at Charlie and I think he sees the confusion in my expression.

"You okay?"

I nod. "See you later, alright?"

He answers with a nod, and watches me as I make my way to my ex. Marc's black hair is neatly trimmed, the way it always is, with that carefully crafted disheveled look. Everything about Marc is stylish and refined. I used to love that about him.

He cuts the rest of the distance and pulls me into a hug, then kisses my cheek. The familiar scent of Ralph Lauren greets me. The whole time, I'm in a trance.

"What are you doing here?"

His eyes soften. I had forgotten how pale they are, like crushed ice.

"I wanted to see you. Is that…okay?"

I eye him for a moment, then nod.

"Wanna go for a drink?"

I say yes and he opens the car door for me. We drive a few blocks to a small restaurant nearby. I'm pleased, because it's probably one of the only places on the island where I haven't been with Jake. We sit at a small table by the window. The whole time Marc makes easy conversation and I half-listen while I rack my brain as to why he's here. I think he sees that in my eyes because his hand reaches for mine over the table.

"I'm here for the weekend. I rented a sailboat. I thought maybe we could spend some time together, the way we used to before it all went to hell. We can talk."

"Marc. I…"

"Come on. Give me two days. We can just be…friends. Are you working tomorrow?"

I shake my head no.

"Say yes. I know you love sailing."

I look out the window. I did…do love sailing. That used to be our thing. We would get on his sailboat and would go away for long weekends at a time, or sometimes just long enough to catch the sunset. We snuggled together, watching the sky darken while we made plans to go around the world.

"Alright." I turn to look at him and his answering smile is dazzling.

We end up having dinner, too. Marc talks about his work projects and I listen, glad with the distraction from my own life. He's with a new agency and is excited about the new accounts he's managing. They are mainly pro athletes and he gets to travel around the world.

Afterwards, he takes me home and we make plans for him to pick me up early the next morning. He's staying at a hotel downtown, and the sailboat he rented is up the coast at the Dana Point marina. I tell him I'm tired and don't invite him in. I'm still not sure how I feel about him being here. I guess I'll have two days to find out.

He pulls me into his arms and buries his nose in my hair. "I miss you, Nati."

I close my eyes, knowing that the next two days will either be one more curveball life throws at me, or a brand new chance.

Chapter 32: *Jake*

I drive to her house most nights after the time Zack branded me with his fist. Switching corners so the neighbors don't call the cops on me, I keep vigil until the late hours. *Great headline, Jake: From Olympic Gold Medalist to Ultimate Stalker.*

Sometimes, I can see her through her windows. She stares outside, and ties her hair up into a knot. She stands there for long periods of time. Other nights she's not home when I get there and I wait, letting the possible scenarios torture me as they go through my head. Her with Charlie, her with someone new. The anxiety grips me until she finally comes home.

She always comes home alone.

Until one night, she doesn't.

Sudden fury surges through me when I watch her step out of a black Maserati followed by that fucker she used to be engaged to. I have to fight the urge to bolt out of the car and ask her what the fuck she thinks she's doing. That asshole is a cheating scumbag. She can do better than him. *Who, Jake? You?* I close my hands into fists.

I don't go back after that night.

Double Post keeps me busy. The surfboards are already on backorder and the sales for custom gear have almost tripled. I really have more than I can chew for now and it's almost enough to keep my brain occupied.

I have to hire more employees and a manager. One of the girls I hire looks at me with puppy-dog eyes, and doesn't miss an opportunity to flirt with me. I have half a mind to tell her this isn't going to work. She asks me out for a drink after we close one night, and I turn her down. In Natalia's words, drinks with the boss *is not a good idea*. She frowns when I tell her, and doesn't ask again.

I call my brother Jamie, and ask if I can come up to Santa Barbara that weekend. I haven't seen him in a while.

When I finally make it up there, he greets me at the door with a hug.

"It's good to see you, Jake. It's been too long this time."

His two boys run to the door and immediately start climbing on me. I grab their arms and throw them on my back. They love it when I do that and giggle till they can't breathe. Jamie's wife, Christina, appears at the door and smiles, then hugs me.

"Jake. We've missed you. Come in."

We have lunch, and the kids run to the pool afterwards. They are only five and seven years old, but Jamie's already teaching them to play water polo. I promise them I'll be out to play after I catch up with Jamie. Christina smiles and leaves behind the boys.

I tell Jamie about Double Post, and about my decision to retire. Jamie knows about my former job as an escort. He's glad to hear I've left that lifestyle, and listens intently. Then without planning to, I tell him about Natalia. I tell him about the day I met her, and how things quickly turned into more.

"It was unstoppable. She changed the way I felt about a lot of things. That's why I ended up retiring. I couldn't do it anymore."

"That's good, Jake. Sounds like she's worth fighting for."

"How did you do it, Jamie? How did you forgive Mom?"

Jamie looks at me for a long moment. "I had to. When I met Christina, it all came back. Just like it happened with you and Natalia. Christina told me she loved me, every day. And after who knows how long, the penny dropped. I wouldn't be able to love anyone until I forgave Mom and let all of that go."

"Just like that?"

"No, Jake. It took a long time. But I did it. I have an amazing family now. You can have that, too."

Jamie's words sink in. As I drive home, the memories from the past haunt me once again, but for the first time, I feel pity for my mother instead of hate. Dad always said she was broken. Maybe he was right.

What I don't know, is if I can be like Jamie, or if I'm as broken as she was.

Chapter 33: *Natalia*

Marc picks me up at six the next morning. We drive for a little over an hour up the coast to the Dana Point marina. He packed enough food for an entire weekend, and makes quick work of loading everything into the sailboat. It is beautiful, twenty-five feet of space we'll be sharing for the next two days. The fog is light today and the wind is slowly picking up. The forecast announced perfect weather, and as we set sail, my nerves rattle.

We immediately fall into our own sailing routine as we make our way across toward Avalon on Catalina Island. Marc is an exceptional sailor. He moves around the sailboat with confidence and ease. I follow his commands and we work in comfortable silence, the way we have done so many times in the past.

By the time we get to Avalon, it's a little after four in the afternoon. The sun is still high, so we decide to walk around the island to explore.

We find an old cantina, have cold beers and fried fish, then go back to the boat to watch the sun disappear behind the island. Despite everything that's happened, it's still easy to be with Marc. He is an innate charmer. He wants to know every detail about my internship, and laughs at my anecdotes about the kitchen and what we had to endure as interns. When I ask him about his job, his face lights up. I used to love listening to Marc talk about work. His mind is brilliant, the ideas flowing nonstop. He tells me about his latest work at the agency, and all the places he's traveled in the last few months. I listen to him talk and smile, remembering the trips we took together. There are so many happy memories in our past: sailing around the Caribbean in a boat like this one, eating fresh shrimp and drinking warm rum on the deck as we watched the sun sink into a collage of magentas and blue.

The wind picks up and I shiver. Mark immediately takes off his sweatshirt and wraps it around me. The eternal gentleman, that was one of my favorite things about him. He doesn't have to think about it, it's part of his DNA. I sit with my back against his chest, and he wraps his arms around me. I close my eyes and breathe in traces of Ralph Lauren mixed with the ocean. It seems strange to be here, like this, after everything that's happened.

"I've missed you, Nati." Marc kisses my head, and when I look up, he dips his face and our lips meet. It's soft, tender, and the taste is familiar. I close my eyes and let the good memories in.

Marc makes love to me in the small cabin, the waves rocking us as they lap against the boat. It's not desperate like it was with Jake. Sex with Jake was savage, a primal thirst that needed to be quenched. Marc is gentle, different, and knows my body well. He pins me under him, sinking in and out of me, his eyes closed. Did he always close his eyes when we made love? I've never noticed it before. Jake's eyes were always locked on mine, so intense. Why am I thinking about Jake now?

Later, I lie awake in Marc's arms for hours while his chest heaves up and down peacefully. It would be easy to fall back into this. Let all the happy memories I have with Marc envelope me. We could start the family we always dreamed of. I could work part time, be a mother. I have always known life with Marc would be stable. I would want for nothing. Is that what I want?

In the morning, we have breakfast at a small café overlooking the bay. The day is crisp, and the wind has picked up, promising an easy ride home. We spend a few hours exploring more of the island. We walk around the Botanical Gardens and visit The Catalina Island Museum. At noon, we eat a quick lunch before setting sail back to Dana Point.

By the time we make it back to my door, it's nearly ten in the evening. It's hard to keep my eyes open. Marc wants to stay the night, and I tell him it's okay, though I need to leave early for work the next morning.

When we make love that night, I close my eyes and don't think. I'm all sensation. Marc kisses every inch of my skin. He lowers himself on top of me, then opens his eyes, searching mine.

"I love you, Natalia."

I bring his mouth to mine and kiss him. I don't say 'I love you' back. I don't say anything. I still love Marc, of course. But I don't know if it will be ever be the same between us. I close my eyes and let him love me, surrendering to the memories of our happy times.

The fresh aroma of coffee wakes me. I have to be at work in an hour, so I quickly rush through my morning routine.

Marc is already in the kitchen, showered and dressed for work. He's tanned from the weekend, and his blue eyes blaze against the russet tone of his skin. A familiar flutter swirls in my stomach. We have a quick breakfast in comfortable silence. I tell him I had a great time. It was good to see him. When I kiss him goodbye, he pulls me into his arms.

"I'm going to England next week. I'll be there for two weeks, then in Germany for one more. Come with me."

Whoa. "What?"

"Come with me." He takes my hands and looks into my eyes. "I love you, Natalia. I want to marry you. Come to England with me as my wife."

I take a step back "Marc. I don't think that's a good idea."

"Why? Because of what happened before?"

"Yes and no. I mean...I just can't."

"Nati." He searches my eyes. "I know I'm an asshole for what I've done to you. I'm *so* sorry. I am. I never wanted to hurt you. I was selfish. I wish I could take it all back, but I can't. What I *can* do is promise you I will never hurt you again."

"Marc. I can't do this now." I fight back the tears. I have a sudden urge to run. This is too much.

"Just promise me you'll think about it, then. I'm in love with you, Natalia. I want to take care of you. Give me another chance." He presses a soft kiss on my lips.

"I have to go to work now. Can we talk about this later?"

"I have to be back in L.A. by noon. It's not complicated, Nati. We had a great weekend. I want you back. We can make this work."

I pull back so I can look in his eyes. "We did have a great weekend. But that's not enough to make a decision about the rest of our lives."

"Okay. Come with me and we'll figure things out while we are away."

"Marc, no. I have job interviews here. I can't leave now."

He watches me for a few moments. "Alright. When I get back then. I'll come over and we can spend the weekend together. We can talk."

"Marc...I...*Shit*. I'm going to be late."

"I know you still love me, Nati."

"It's not that simple. I want other things, too."

"Okay. Like what?"

"I want to start my career. I want to find a job and stay in San Diego."

"Nati. Come on." He pulls back a strand of my hair and tucks it behind my ear. "My job is in L.A. We don't have to go back to the Manhattan Beach house. I'll sell it and we can buy another house together. You can find work anywhere you want."

"You're not listening to me, Marc. I don't want to live in Los Angeles."

"Okay, look. We can work something out," he says, pulling me back into his arms. "You're the most important thing to me right now. I will do whatever it takes, Nati. I love you. We can have it all back. We can make our future. Whatever we want, travel, kids. You can open a little shop on the beach. I want you to be happy. Just think about it, okay? Let's talk when I come back from Europe."

"Marc. I…"

He doesn't let me finish and pulls me back into his arms.

"What can I do? What do you need from me?"

I press my face against his chest. "Space and time, I guess."

He squeezes me hard and kisses my head. "Okay."

On my way to work, I replay my weekend with Marc in my head. He's given me more good memories to add to the old ones. Maybe he's right, and we can make things work. I may even be able to forgive the cheating, leave that behind. I love him. But deep inside, I also know things between Marc and me are different now.

Maybe that's a good thing.

Do I want a new start with Marc? Or is it time to finally let go...

As the week comes to an end, the kitchen staff throws a party for all the interns. Everybody is in a great mood. Charlie will begin his new position Monday, and I tease him that he will miss me more than he thinks. He takes my face in his hands and his blue eyes are soft.

"Of course, I'll miss you. The hoax will be up within a day. They'll know I'm only talented when you and I work side by side." He gives me a soft peck on the cheek and I blush. I will miss Charlie.

Later, we all meet downtown for drinks. Even Chef Pierre comes to celebrate with the staff. I hug him and thank him for everything he's done for me. He asks me if I have any more interviews, and I tell him I had two more with the hotel in Del Mar and I'm hoping they will call. He smiles.

By one in the morning, my head is heavy and I want to go home. I have another interview tomorrow and need to get some sleep. I wait at the curb for a cab. The first thing I'll do if I get a job is lease or buy a car. San Diego is not like Buenos Aires when it comes to public transportation, and it can take most of the day to get from one place to the next. It's crazy. I would spend most of my salary on cab rides.

In the morning, my phone rings as I'm waiting for the taxi that will take me to the interview at a hotel downtown. My heart stills when I recognize the number of the hotel in Del Mar.

Hannah from Human Resources tells me they're prepared to offer me a job as a sous chef. My heart is banging so hard against my chest I wonder if Hannah can hear it. I still have several interviews at other places, but this was my top choice. I know Chef Pierre has most likely called in a personal favor since he's close friends with the executive chef there. Hannah tells me to come in the next day to get a tour of the kitchen. I call the hotel where I was about to have the interview, and tell them I accepted another job.

The next morning, I meet with the executive chef and he introduces me to the rest of the kitchen staff. After that, I sit down with Hannah and she presents me with a formal offer. I accept it on the spot. I really don't need to think about this any longer.

In the afternoon, I wander listlessly around my apartment. Marc has respected the time I've asked him for, and hasn't called.

For the first time in a long while, I think about Jake. Tomorrow is his birthday and I wonder who he will spend it with. Did he move on?

I think of all the things Jake and I went through, and the new possibilities Marc offered me.

My head spins.

Despite the chaos, there are two things I do know.

What Jake and I had was real.

But what Marc and I can build together is full of promise as well.

Chapter 34: *Jake*

Even after two days, the image of Natalia and her ex is still branded in my mind. Why would she go back to that fucker? The thought that she's already moved on torments me.

When I walk into Double Post, Grayson, the new manager I hired, greets me with a smile. He's the epitome of a surfer: long bleached hair, baked skin, and an easy smile. Not much gets in the way of Grayson's untroubled demeanor. The amount of female customers has almost doubled since he started working here. I like him. He's always in a good mood and keeps things light.

"Morning, boss. What's happening?"

"Good morning, Grayson," I mutter. Unlike Grayson, my moods roam at sea level. At the front counter, I scroll down the computer screen, scanning through yesterday's transactions.

"Didn't tell me it was your birthday, dude."

I look up at him and frown. I didn't tell anyone it was my birthday today.

"I told Pete to keep his mouth shut. Do the same, Grayson." I focus back on the screen.

"Pete didn't spill, man. The hot chick that was here this morning gave it away."

This gets my attention. Hot chick? *Shit*. Pete introduced me to one of their new instructors at the club. I haven't gone out with anyone since Natalia, and I'm not fucking interested. I curse Pete for telling her it was my birthday.

"She left you something." Grayson smiles and gestures to my office. I shake my head. *Fuck*. Now I'm going to have to call her.

I push away from the desk and rub my forehead as I make the short way to my office. Grayson smiles and leaves to the back.

There is a white box on my desk. It's not wrapped. Just a plain white cardboard box with a wide silk white ribbon around it. No card either. I pull the ribbon and when I open the box the aroma of fresh cookies hits me. I lift up the tissue paper and my chest constricts.

The box is full of those cookies Natalia used to make for me. *Alfajores*. I remember telling her I wanted them for my birthday. She sent me a whole box of them. There is a small white card on top. It simply says Happy Birthday. She didn't sign it. She didn't have to.

I'm tripping. Is she thinking of me, or was this one of those sweet things she used to do all the time?

I have to find out.

That night Syd and Pete have me over for dinner. Syd even baked me a chocolate cake. I don't tell them about the cookies. Since Natalia and I broke up, I've respected her friendship with Sydney by not asking questions. I didn't want to fuck that up for her, too.

We finish dinner, and Syd leaves to put baby Mia down. Pete opens two beers, then plops down on the couch across from me.

"Natalia stopped by Double Post today." I keep my eyes on him as I take a long sip of beer.

He frowns. "What for?"

"She brought me a box of cookies."

"Oh, yeah?"

"I told her once it was what I wanted for my birthday."

Pete nods once, eyeing me.

"Tell me, man. Is she with someone?"

He shrugs. "I don't know, Jake. Why don't you ask her?"

"Don't be an asshole."

He smiles. "Syd doesn't tell me anything, man."

"Just tell me one thing. Did she get back together with that fucker? Her ex?"

Pete frowns. "I told you I don't know, so stop asking."

"You know, I keep racking my brain to figure out exactly when everything turned south. I think it was when Dillon said he was moving down to Argentina. Fucker."

Pete nods. "She probably realized everyone else was moving forward except you two," he says matter-of-factly. "You can't blame her, Jake. You had to know that was going to happen sooner or later."

I scowl at him. "Why? We had a good thing going. No broken promises, no plans that would've been abandoned later on."

"Jake. You can't seriously tell me you expected to keep it going forever. What the fuck, man? You can't build anything without compromise. You have to be willing to take a fucking risk."

"I'm not like you, Pete. I'm not cut out that way."

"Why? Because of what your mother did to you a million years ago? No offense, man. But you need to stop living in the past and fucking get over it."

I glare at him. Pete is the only person that can get away with talking to me this way. I would have beat the shit out of anyone else for even bringing up my past, and Pete's throwing it in my face.

"It's not something you can just get over, Pete," I mutter.

"Yes. It is. And it's your decision, Jake."

I let my head hang and blow out a deep breath. "Shit, man. It's too late for an intervention. I've fucked everything up."

"So go fix it."

"She said she loved me. It scares the shit out of me."

"So what? It scares all of us, Jake. You just have to go for it."

"I don't know, man. I don't know how to give her what she wants."

"She wanted *you*, Jake. That's all she's ever wanted. Offer Natalia a future, man. It's the only way out of this, even for you. Until you let go of the past you will be a fucking slave to your own demons. I know what your mom did to you was cold as fuck, but you've got to let it go, man."

"Why would she want me, Pete? I'm nothing but a goddamn whore."

Pete leans forward on his seat. When I look up at him, his eyes are blazing. "That's not how I see you. That's not how any of us see you. You're a fucking gold medal Olympian, Jake. You're my hero, man. Don't ever say to me that you're not worth it."

I slump against the back of the couch and stare at the ceiling. My head is about to explode, and it's doing a damn good job at trying to override the mammoth foot on my chest. A few silent minutes go by. Pete rubs the back of his head and lets out a sigh.

"Jake you're like a brother to me and I love you. But if you don't go and fix things with Natalia, you're a bigger asshole than I thought."

"Fuck. I wouldn't even know where to start."

"Tell her you love her."

I glare up at him. The panic rises from my chest and I push it down.

"Say it." Pete's eyes lock on mine, but I don't look away. I close my hands into fists to stop them from trembling as the darkness threatens to take over.

"Jake. For fuck's sake. Admit that you love her. That's step one.

"*Say it*, man!" he snaps and I jump. I stand up and pace the room like a caged tiger. Pete is right. I have to win against the past, or it will swallow me. I stand by the window, squeezing the back of my neck as I stare at the pitch black of the ocean. Pete's hand grips my shoulder and he searches my eyes. He's looking at me like he thinks maybe I can't do this. Then his expression changes and his mouth curves up at the corner.

"Think of it as a ball game."

I narrow my eyes. Pete knows me better than anyone. If this is a game, then I *have* to win. I swallow the boulder in my throat.

"I love her. I've loved her from the first time I saw her." Instant relief washes through me. It's a fucking surprise that leaves me speechless. Pete pulls me into an embrace, patting my back.

"That's right, brother. That's step one." He smiles. "Now go get her, man."

"It's been two months, Pete. She may not want anything to do with me."

Pete grins. "My money is on you, Jake. They don't give gold medals to people that come in second."

"You have an answer for everything, asshole. What do you suggest I do?"

"Get back in the game and fight, man. Get back in the game and fight."

Chapter 35: *Natalia*

I spend the morning running errands and picking up the rest of my things from work before I start my new job on Monday. I pack everything into a backpack and say goodbye to the last of the kitchen staff. The day is beautiful, so I take my time walking home. It is almost lunchtime, and I debate whether or not to get something to eat, then decide against it. My savings are scant and I need to be frugal until I get my first real paycheck. I tread along, thinking how much I will miss living in Coronado. My new job will mean a half an hour commute, and I need to find an apartment that is closer.

When I get home, I take the stairs two at a time, wondering what I have in the fridge. I unlock the door, then freeze because I have somehow walked into the wrong apartment.

I step out, then back into, what up until this afternoon, was my living room.

It is now filled with flowers.

Everywhere.

White roses to be precise. I look around the room in shock. It's like a scene from a movie. There are large and small vases with flowers on every surface of my small living room. They are stunning. And they're also my favorite flowers.

What the hell?

"Your landlady let me in. It took some persuading, but...as it turns out, I can be pretty persuasive."

I whip around and Jake is standing behind me. Holy shit. My heart has a ninja fit inside my chest.

"Jake. What...Did you do this?"

He nods.

I look back at the white cloud of roses. "There are so many." A knot swells in my throat and my eyes are starting to sting from the moisture that is pooling in them. I clutch my jacket to hold back the tears, but one escapes. Jake walks around me, then smiles as he wipes my cheek with his thumb.

"There is one flower here for every day that I've known and loved you, Natalia. One hundred and seventy two, to be exact."

I stop breathing. Did he just say...?

"Yes," he says, answering my unspoken question. I have loved you every day since I first saw you. I was just too blind to see it. All this time, I thought that if we kept things in the present, neither of us would ever get hurt. But I was wrong. I'm sorry." He wipes another stray tear from my cheek. "I'm sorry for all the times I made you cry. And for all the times that I left your apartment without telling you how much I was looking forward to the next time I saw you. And for not telling you about retiring sooner, I know now how insensitive that was on my part."

"Jake..."

"Shhh. Let me finish." He wraps his arms around me and I'm glad, because I cannot take any more of this. He presses his forehead to mine. "I want to be able to tell you every day how much I love you, and how great my life is because you're in it. I want your present and I also want your future, Natalia. And I want you to be legally required to wake up in my bed every morning. Will you marry me?" He pulls away to look into my eyes. They are wide and I'm completely speechless. He smiles.

"Don't leave me hanging."

I blink a few times through the shock. "Jake. That's...a very generous offer and I can only imagine how hard it was for you to say that. It means a lot, but I got a job this week. The hotel will take care of my visa. You don't need to..."

He gives me a lopsided smile. "That's not what I meant when I said 'legally required to wake up in my bed.' And this isn't hard for me at all. In fact, it's the easiest decision I've ever had to make. I want to make plans with you, Natalia. Plans for the future that we follow or we change together. I love you, Nati. Please just...say yes."

The tears are flowing down my cheeks on their own accord and the words are trapped in my throat. Jake scoops me up and squeezes me in his arms.

"What do you think?" he says softly.

I smile and lean my forehead on his.

"Jake Harper, I think that's a very good idea."

FIN.

Epilogue: *Natalia*

From under my umbrella, I watch Jake walk back from the ocean with this surfboard under his arm. His golden skin glistens under the afternoon sun. He shakes the water off his hair. He's beautiful. He's mine.

The ocean used to remind me of Marc. Now, it's one more new memory of Jake and I together.

Saying goodbye to Marc was not easy. Despite the pain he once caused me, I didn't want to hurt him. There is a part of me that will always love Marc. But when I saw Jake at my apartment that morning, the morning of the flowers...it is true what they say about true love.

When you know, you know.

Jake and I had a small wedding at the beach a few months after his proposal. We only invited our closest friends. It was fun and intimate, just like we both wanted.

Double Post has become a Cardiff icon. People come from all over California to meet Jake and his surfboards are on constant backorder. Jake is happier than I have ever seen him.

My job at the Del Mar hotel under Chef Antoine is demanding, but much more gratifying than I even imagined. Chef Antoine has a fiery temper, but I don't let it get to me and continue to work hard. He doesn't give praise easily, but I think I'm doing okay because he's slowly letting me in on his techniques and years of experience. I'm very lucky to work at his side. Chef Pierre has come to visit at work and seemed impressed with my progress. He keeps telling Antoine he will steal me when he's not looking. My dream to open my own pastry shop is getting closer. Jake helps me with the planning and it's beginning to seem real. We are both keeping our ears to the ground for retail space that may become available in Cardiff.

Dani and Dillon are engaged. It is good to see my friend in love and, even though she and Dillon haven't said anything, I wouldn't be surprised if they ended up in California. Hopefully not too far from us. Zack is dating a marketing director in Buenos Aires. She's in awe of his talent, and wants to help him open his own place.

I have met Jake's brother Jamie and his family. They have welcomed me warmly and I make sure we see them at least once a month. I love being a part of their life, and that they're now a big part of mine.

Pete and Sydney are expecting another baby. A boy.

Jake wants to have a baby soon. I want a family with Jake, but I want us to have time together first. There is still a lot we don't know about each other and I'm liking the discovery stage of our relationship. Living my life without a perfectly planned future is a new adventure. I have always needed to know exactly where I was going. But I have to admit, that building a future with Jake every day is a lot more fun. I take what life brings me and am no longer afraid I will lose the people I love. Love finally made it all the way into my heart.

And I will never let it go.

FIN (For real!)

Acknowledgements:

So many people have participated in one way or another in the creation of this book. Tiny pixels of support, wisdom, information, or simply by conveying your belief that I could make it happen. Huge thanks to all of you out there.

You know who you are.

A special hug to my guardian angel of dreams, Marilyn.

I would have never gotten this far, had it not been for you fueling my creative monster.

To my husband and three kids, for the hours of listening to my ramble of ideas and thoughts, and for giving me tight hugs when I gave up hope.

Your support is the best gift I could have wished for.

A very special hug to my family and friends in Argentina.

All believers.

All fans from day one.

Even before you read a word.

You rock.

Lastly, but not least, special thanks to all my friends who read bits or drafts of my work in progress and made it better: Roberta, Julie, Maureen, Anne, Inga, Jen, Elise, a huge hug to you all. And my friend Mike, for his endless patience and wisdom when it came to my technical issues.

Until the next one...

<u>Other Titles by J. Q. Anderson</u>

Kings of Midnight: Book One of the Midnight Saga (Published 2020)

Read the first chapter at the end of this book.

Ghost of Dawn: Book Two of the Midnight Saga (Coming 2021).

About J.Q. Anderson

J. Q. Anderson is a debut author who loves stories of all kinds, cooking food from her home town, Argentina, and hanging out with friends and family. When she's not working, she's writing relentlessly, or hanging out with her husband and three kids.

Writing is a multi-faceted passion. You're in love with making stuff that wasn't there before. You think, you create, you obsess, and then you obsess a little more. Before the words even get to the page they have been roaming in all corners of your mind, trying to shape themselves.

I would have never dared to write a word had it not been for the people that love and suck in those stories.

To all the crazies out there, I hope you enjoy my attempt at making you travel to a faraway land.

Kings of Midnight: Book One of the Midnight Saga

Chapter 1

That morning, the morning of the pointe shoe and the speeding car, the morning I met Him, didn't start any differently. Life chuckled at me from above, nothing tipping me off on how it was about to mess with me.

Big time.

I held my half-eaten toast between my teeth as I pushed open the foyer door while shrugging into my parka. Strapping my dance bag across my back, I hurried through the streets of downtown Buenos Aires. The damp air from an earlier rain filled my lungs as I jogged—away from work—steam building inside my parka. *You don't have time for this*, my roommate's voice rang in my head. *You'll be late. Again.* But on a rebellious—and childish, I admit—impulse, I was doing it anyway. Even though I knew she was right. Even though that morning in particular I should have been at work early because the artistic director would be posting the casting for my favorite ballet, *Giselle*.

I had exactly twenty minutes to pick up my much-awaited custom pointe shoes and make it to the theater on time, or I would get grilled by my teacher, Madame Vronsky.

My feet complained from the long hours en pointe, but even after a year with the company, I still felt a high as I rushed to work every morning. Being part of the permanent ballet of the Colón Theater was every Argentinean dancer's ultimate dream and, in my case, also the first step toward my future career as a prima in New York City. New York was the grand prize for me, a future far away from Buenos Aires and the shadow of my own mother's brilliant career as the country's most beloved prima ballerina.

I rang the doorbell of the old building, catching my breath. Anna's small frame appeared almost immediately, as if she had been waiting behind the door.

"Camila, darling. Come on in," she said, ushering me inside and away from the morning chill.

"Sorry to come so early, but my schedule's crazy. I have no free time anymore."

I followed her into the small foyer, and the familiar smell of wood polish welcomed me. She reached into an armoire I had always believed was magic. It was neatly stocked with Anna's irreproducible works of art. I let my bag drop to the floor, watching impatiently while she retrieved the treasure I had been dreaming of for days: a pair of her special edition, hand-embroidered pointe shoes. I took them in my hands and grinned. Closing my eyes, I pressed them to my nose and inhaled my favorite smell in the world: satin and leather.

"They're beautiful," I whispered. And they were. Pale pink satin from Italy, carefully embroidered with the finest silk threads in elaborate patterns. Nobody made ballet shoes like Anna. At seventy years old, she still ran her own workshop. The wait list was normally several months long, but I had lucked out because

Anna was my mother's favorite ballet shoemaker during her days as a prima. It also didn't hurt that my father was Anna's doctor and she had him on a sky-high pedestal. So as soon as I had asked her, Anna had squeezed my order in. I handed her the money I had been saving for the last three months and kissed her tissue-soft cheek. "You're the best, Anna. I gotta run. Take care, okay?"

"Let me get a sack for you. These are more delicate than your regular shoes. You don't want to put them in your bag with all your other things. The fabric is pure silk, it stains easily."

"I'll carry them in my hands. I need to go, okay? You don't have to get me a sack."

"No, no. One more minute won't matter."

Wanna bet?

"The new girl moves my things around. It's driving me crazy." She browsed through one, two, three drawers.

"Anna…" I fidgeted. Jesus, at this pace, Madame would have my head.

"Ah. Here." She opened a pale pink silk bag, and I quickly slid the shoes in, then followed her to the front door where, with unhurried movements, she eased the lock. "Say hello to your parents for me, will you?"

"Will do, Anna. *Chau*." I dashed out, shouldering my ballet bag as I clutched the precious sack in both hands, flexing the shoes back and forth. I couldn't wait to try them on. Before wearing them, I would have to go through the whole ritual of breaking them in: bend them, buff the points to give them grip, pull out the inseams, and quarter the shanks to mold them to my feet. All without damaging the precious embroidery.

Needles of wind prickled my cheeks while I waited at the traffic light to cross 9 de Julio, Buenos Aires's iconic avenue, the widest in the world. The city's pulse quickened, a sulky dragon waking from a too-short slumber. I pulled the shoes out of the bag and admired them. Holding them in my hand, I darted a quick look at the now green light and hurried across the massive width of pavement. A passing body bumped my shoulder. I was almost at the other side when a woman in a crisp suit heading my way pointed behind me.

"*Querida*, you dropped something."

Instinctively, my fist tightened on the one—shit!—shoe I was holding. I whipped my head around and my heart constricted. The other shoe lay innocently a third of the way behind, a small wedge of pink on a sea of asphalt. Shit. That shoe was unique, and it cost a big chunk of my salary, plus the waiting time. My eyes flew to the light.

Adrenaline surged through me as I sprinted, every one of my limbs tensing to win the race against the tidal wave of incoming traffic. Without pausing, I bent down, scraping my fingers against the asphalt, and hooked the rim of the slipper. Behind me, an explosion of horns blasted, and I tripped forward with my hands tightly clutching the shoes. I squeezed my eyes shut, bracing for the impact, but the force of a tornado scooped me up and whirled me away.

"Are you *insane*?" snarled a deep, husky voice that went with the tornado.

I blinked through the shock, panting. As the world came into focus, my brain registered the pair of ash-colored eyes locked on mine. They were wide with annoyance, yet absolutely stunning, a cloud of powder blue, or was it silver?

"What the hell?" he said, now sounding less annoyed and more concerned.

"What?" I muttered, still trying to pin the exact color of his eyes.

"Did you seriously almost kill yourself for a *shoe*?"

Reality hit at once and I straightened out of his muscular arms, clutching the pointe shoes in my hands. *Safe.* "These are important," I murmured, securing them inside my bag that was somehow still tucked under my arm. I took an unstable step, and a shard of fire burned through my ankle. Shit. Not now. I let out a tense breath, clenching my teeth at the old injury. Nothing I couldn't handle. But the slightest twitch in the wrong direction could make the day's rehearsals unbearable. Pain shot up my leg when I took another step, and I winced.

"You hurt your ankle." He grabbed my arm gently, his tone impatient.

"Yes, but no," I said, cringing at the pain. I had no time for any of this. I looked up at him to send him off but stopped as I fully took in his appearance. Rebellious strands of raven hair framed the angular, perfect features of his face. His eyes narrowed a fraction, the furious silver of his irises blazing against sun-kissed, olive skin. A soft, five-o'clock stubble shadowed the square lines of his jaw. *Damn.* He was fucking beautiful. A mix between a superhero and something darker, an X-Man. My heart stuttered.

"I'm fine," I muttered, shaking off the trance. A sudden panic struck me, and I glanced down at my watch. Shit. I was late for the cast meeting. I flinched inwardly at the thought of Madame scolding me for my tardiness. I would much rather deal with my throbbing ankle than her. But as I took a step, pain burned through my ankle. I groaned in frustration.

"Here," he said. "Don't put your full weight on it." He held my arm gently and arranged it over his for support. I opened my mouth to protest, but when I took a step, the pain was significantly less. This was helping. "Careful." He pressed me against him to let a guy having a heated phone conversation pass us by. My whole body shivered at the closer contact with him. "This city's forgotten its manners," he murmured, looking down at me. Concern flashed in his eyes when he saw me frowning, though it wasn't at him, but at the sudden hormonal frenzy inside me.

"You okay?" The deep, raspy tone of his voice rippled through me, and I nodded. What was this? I didn't let myself swoon. Not even by ridiculously hot guys like this one. I didn't have time.

"I'm late," I said, pulling him with me to keep the weight off my ankle as I hurried.

"Will you slow down?" His hand clasped my arm more firmly. It was a bit comical: me half limping and him holding me to slow me down.

"I can't," I blurted. I darted a desperate look at him, and he was smiling in resignation. A small dimple had formed on his cheek. It was sexy and adorable. Dammit, I didn't like that he was so good-looking. It made me nervous. Yet, I was strangely enjoying his persistence and unnecessary concern for my safety. "You really don't need to escort me."

"Guarding instincts are intact. That's good. Come on." He nodded.

Arguing with him was wasted time. Plus, he gave long strides and we were moving fast. I let myself relax a fraction, using his arm as support as we navigated through a thickening mass of morning workers who seemed to have just realized they were going to be late for work.

"What's your name, crazy girl?"

"I'm *not* crazy. That shoe is one of a kind. And it costs a fortune."

"I can only imagine if you were willing to kill yourself for it."

"You ran into the street too."

"I did. To save *you.*"

I thought about that as we awkwardly limped and hurried, dodging bodies in suits. He seemed at ease, as if going out of his way to help a complete stranger wasn't a nuisance at all. Didn't *he* have a boss? I was grateful, though. My ankle was warming up and already felt stronger. I would have to wrap it up before class, but it would be okay.

We stopped at the last light, and he pulled me closer. I resented the way my stomach swam at the heavenly scent of his body wash. He was tall. I peeked up at him and our eyes met. His were simply breathtaking. Like they had come up with their own color and didn't give a shit if it existed or not. Everything about him was confidence.

"Thank you," I said—I realized—for the first time.

He nodded.

"I'm fine now." I pulled my arm away gently. "Work's right over there. I'm good."

"You sure?"

I glanced at the theater doors as Karina and Paula ran in. They were always late. Crap. I set off to cross even though the light was still red, but his hand was quicker and gripped my arm tightly, growling as a car blazed by.

"Christ, girl. You *are* crazy," he barked.

I pulled my arm away. "I'm *not* crazy. I can't be late."

He clutched my elbow, forcing me to stop. His eyes pinned me down with a stern glare. "*Nothing* is worth getting killed for."

"You haven't met my teacher."

He shook his head in exasperation, and I let myself smile at the small victory as I glanced at the *still goddamn red* light.

"Really my work is just across the street," I said. "You can brag to your friends over how you saved a crazy girl from her death. Now go, I don't want to make you late for work."

He studied me for a second and ran a hand through his hair, a beautiful mess in perfect disarray, and I wished I hadn't noticed those tanned, roped arms under rolled-up sleeves. His mouth curved into a lopsided smile, and a million butterflies I didn't know existed inside my stomach fluttered their wings. *God.*

"All right. Be safe, okay? It was nice meeting you, crazy girl."

I blushed furiously, and my usual steel armor suddenly felt like a child's paper costume. I nodded, and forgetting about my ankle, I bolted to the theater entrance, desperate to escape him and the tornado of sensations whirling inside my rib cage.

To be continued...